BELLA'S CHRISTMAS BLUNDER

A Sugar Plum Romance

DARCI BALOGH

CHAPTER 1

Early in the morning on the first day of December, Bella Velez stood on a sidewalk in New York City staring across the street. Staring at a building to be exact. Her building.

She had waited years for this day, 15 years, and her dreams had finally come true. She could hardly believe that at long last she was looking at her very own New York restaurant.

A freezing wind bit her cheeks and nose, but the rest of her was thoroughly bundled in a pure white wool coat with oversized black buttons. With her long brown hair tucked underneath a fuzzy black winter hat and most of her face wrapped in a matching scarf, Bella was warm enough. In fact, she was growing hotter and hotter with every passing moment.

She had come straight from the airport after spending the last several weeks with her mother in Spain. An unavoidable trip. Bella's mother had needed her to help with an unexpected illness. Thankfully, her mother was completely recovered, but the long trip had taken a chunk out of the vital weeks before Bella's trendy eatery, Total, opened to the public.

Total, pronounced 'toe-tall', was the culmination of everything Bella had always aspired to in her culinary career. A new beginning in a life that had taken unexpected turns. Some good and many bad. Total was not only to be her job, it was her heart and soul.

Finally standing in front of the beautiful old three story building she had carefully chosen to lease for her restaurant, Bella stared unblinkingly at the signage. Incensed anger bubbled in her stomach and spread up into her chest.

"What happened?" she asked in disbelief.

Nobody was near enough to hear her question. A few street vendors setting up their stands about halfway down the block were chatting and a smattering of pedestrians moved with purpose towards unknown destinations. Other than that, Bella was completely alone.

Alone and trembling. Frustrated and indignant.

She paced back and forth a few steps, barely noticing the biting wind or the cracks in the concrete sidewalk as she mumbled under her breath, "I cannot believe this. The stupidity! Why didn't anyone tell me?"

Taking a deep breath and letting it out slowly, Bella stopped pacing and turned to face her restaurant once more, bracing herself for bitter disappointment again, hoping against hope that she had overreacted the first time.

"No, it's still there," she said out loud. So loud the street vendors glanced curiously in her direction.

The 'it' she was referring to was the sign for Total, which she had specially commissioned and had mounted while she was in Spain. The sign spelled out T-o-t-a-l in beautiful twisting letters. White lettering on a black background with a gold border that added an extra edge of dimension and class. It was perfect. Exactly what she wanted.

However, as her gaze slid to the right of her beautiful new sign there was another new and unexpected sign mounted on the very edge of the building. A sign that used to be a tasteful image of a white cup of coffee with steam rising out of it to signify the small corner coffee shop that occupied that space. A sign that was no longer the coffee cup she remembered, but rather a garish red and blue neon sign blinking obnoxiously in the early morning light. A sign that spelled out in caps, large and comical, 'P-I-T-S'.

Pits? What in the world was a Pits?!

In truth, Bella could care less *what* it was. The thing that was giving her a mini-panic attack was *where* it was. To her dismay when she looked at the building from across the street the signs were positioned so close together that they appeared to announce to the world that the name of her restaurant was 'Total Pits'.

This was a nightmare.

Maybe it was merely an optical illusion from her particular vantage point. Bella hurried to another section of sidewalk on the corner and looked again. Nope. The signs still looked like one sign. One weird sign naming her lifelong dream New York eatery Total Pits.

Mumbling maniacally under her breath, Bella stomped down the block in the other direction, straight by the street vendors who exchanged a look as she passed.

"No, no, no," she said when she stopped at the far corner and turned, only to see the same problem. "All the way down here!" No matter where she stood on the street, near or far, her beautiful, elegant, perfect restaurant looked like it had been christened the ridiculous name Total Pits. Bella was so angry she could cry.

Weeks of endless searching for the perfect spot had brought her to this building. It was an amazing building. Three stories of old brick painted a tasteful grey. Accented by carved wooden window treatments and a strong, elegant cornice held up by beautifully crafted curling brackets, all painted a shining ebony. The exterior of the building had taken her breath away. Not to mention the interior, which was equally satisfying with gleaming wood floors, exposed brick walls, and expensive chandelier lighting.

Bella had been so overcome with delight at finding the perfect place for her restaurant that she had barely thought about the tiny coffee shop in the minuscule corner spot right next to her. A tasteful wine store was on the other side and the rest of the block held a well known cobbler's shop and a stationery store. Nothing to be concerned about.

She had not seen this Pits thing coming, whatever it was, and she didn't know what she was going to do about it. Her feet seemed stuck to the sidewalk as she tried to catch her breath and calm down.

"You all right, doll?" One of the street vendors had stepped away from his brightly decorated cart and moved closer to her.

He looked to be mid-50's, thickly built with short greying hair. He wore a bright red apron with a Santa Claus face on the front over his heavy black jacket. His cart was draped with Christmas lights and thin notes of The First Noel drifted from somewhere inside of it.

Bella tried to gather herself. With a quick shake of her head she answered, "I'm fine."

He shrugged apologetically. "Well, pardon me sayin' so, but you don't exactly look fine." His New York accent was thick.

"I don't?" Bella knew he was right, of course. She felt like screaming or bursting out crying. She shook her head again, trying to regain control of her emotions. "I'm just—there's nothing—it's probably jet lag."

He continued to look at her like he was her wise old uncle

for a few long moments. Then he turned and went quickly back to his cart, grabbed something and brought it back.

"Maybe you need to eat something," he said, holding out a breakfast sandwich wrapped in white paper.

"Oh, no thank you," Bella tried to brush him off. "I don't have any cash."

He waved away her comment. "It's on the house."

She tried to protest again, but the warm sandwich was already in her hand and the man was walking back to his cart. Her stomach growled as the smell of egg and cheese and bacon lifted from the small package. Maybe she did need to eat something.

"Thank you," she said to his back. He merely lifted one arm and waved without turning back to look at her.

Bella breathed in again to get another whiff of her breakfast sandwich. When she did, she noticed a different delectable scent. Baking bread.

She glanced at the street vendors. Their small carts weren't equipped with ovens. She looked up and down the street, but there were no bakeries or bodegas to speak of in the few surrounding blocks.

Her eyes fell on the blinking Pits sign. The lights were on, though it didn't appear to be open to customers yet. Could that be who was baking bread?

No time like the present to find out.

Invigorated by the possibility of dealing with the whole signage issue right away, Bella stepped into the street. As she did, she turned quickly and waved at the friendly street vendor, "Thanks, again."

He smiled and waved back, calling out to her as she hurried across the street, "You're welcome...and try to cheer up, doll. It's almost Christmas!"

CHAPTER 2

The door to Pits pushed open with a cheery jingle and Bella was hit with a blast of warm air heavy with the irresistible smell of fresh baked bread. Her cheeks and fingertips tingled at the instant warmth and her mouth watered automatically at the scent.

A leather strap holding a dozen brass sleigh bells was looped over the inside doorknob, thus the musical accompaniment when the door opened. The floor was the same vintage black and white checked tile that Bella remembered from the coffee shop, but that was the only similarity Pits held to the previous establishment. Transformed into some kind of tiny outlandish blue collar cafe she barely recognized it as the same space.

A long glass counter like those found in a deli had been put in on one side, presumably to allow customers to watch someone make their sandwich. Five tiny bistro tables, all painted with splashes of paint using all of the vibrant colors of the rainbow, were pushed against the outside wall with a view out the single long window. The exposed brick wall this place shared with hers was adorned with three floor to ceiling paintings of neon night scapes on black canvases.

Bella had a few moments to take it all in without interruption as there was nobody manning the counter. Curious, she looked for a menu, but didn't see one on the wall. The only indication of what kind of food Pits planned on selling were plastic squeeze bottles full of a deep red sauce on each table. Hamburgers.

"Hello?" Bella called out. No answer so she stepped further into the restaurant. "Anybody here?" Still no answer. She moved deeper in, towards the back where she assumed the stock room and restrooms existed. "Hello?" Nothing.

At the back of the long deli counter she came upon two doors. One had a square window and a white plaque bolted to it that read 'STAFF ONLY' in bold black letters. She peeped into the window and saw the shining stainless steel surfaces of a quiet kitchen. It was deserted.

A familiar song drifted from somewhere even deeper in the building and her attention was drawn to the second door, also closed. This door was solid wood and had its own sign. Hand drawn in Sharpie on a piece of white card stock paper, the sign pinned to the door read 'Lava Pit'. From the top of the letters shot badly drawn flames in cartoonish disarray.

Bella placed her hand on the knob and pressed her ear to the door to better hear the song. Bluesy music and a voice she knew she had heard before sang a Christmas song, but not a traditional one. Another voice joined in. A live voice. A man was singing along somewhere in the basement.

Bella glanced at the hand written sign as she turned the knob and pushed the door open revealing an ancient wooden staircase leading into the basement. The smell of baking bread nearly knocked her over and the music, much louder now that the door was open, she realized was an Eagles song. An Eagles' Christmas song.

"Please come home for Christmas..." the man sang from the depths of the basement.

"Hello?" Bella tried again even though she knew the music was much too loud for anyone to hear her at the top of the stairs. No surprise that the man just kept singing. She had to go downstairs to get his attention. The lights were on, it smelled delicious, and whoever was downstairs seemed to be in a festive mood, so she decided it wasn't completely creepy or strange for her to make her way down the steps.

As she reached the bottom, she paused. The scene in front of her wasn't creepy, but it did stop her in her tracks.

A tall man stood with his back to her. He faced a brick oven that looked like it had been built into the original brickwork of the building. He pushed a long wooden paddle with fresh risen rolls into the oven, which she knew would bake them to near perfection. Brick ovens created delicious bread.

Long tables filled the space around him. One held beautifully browned rolls that matched those he had just put in to bake. Another table was covered with small balls of dough apparently rising in the warmth. And warm it was.

The heat from the oven created so much of a temperature difference from the bitter cold weather outside and even the cozy atmosphere of the dining room upstairs that Bella's wool jacket already felt weighty and hot.

None of this was a surprise to her. She had been in countless bakeries and even several located underneath the restaurant where they produced fresh baked goods for the menu. Bella wasn't lingering at the foot of the stairs because she was surprised there was a bakery in the basement. She was lingering because the sight of the Christmas carol singing man had left her speechless.

Tall, at least 6'4" if not taller, with worn jeans that fit slightly loose, accentuating the lean muscles of his waist and back, he was an impressive sight. She couldn't help but stare because he had taken his shirt off in the steamy basement leaving only a tight white cotton tank top to show off his physique. Her eyes traveled up from his lower back and followed the line of his body, which V'd out into wide shoulders and long arms that were tightly roped with more muscles. Deltoids and biceps flexing, he grasped the handle of the wooden paddle and sang into it like it was a microphone, "It's the time of year to be with the one you love..."

A smile tugged at Bella's lips as she watched his enthusiastic performance. He was good, actually. His singing skills came in a close second to his dancing and the sensual swing of his hips as he moved to the music.

She liked him immediately, which was interesting because she knew nothing about him. The joy he obviously found in singing and dancing along to Christmas music said a lot. Then there was the fact that he wore a Santa hat. The bright red hat trimmed with white sat jauntily on what looked like sandy blonde hair.

Industrial shelving along the staircase where she stood held buckets, bags, and boxes of restaurant supplies and partially hid her from his view. Tucked neatly at the bottom of the stairs, Bella could have happily watched him for a bit longer, appreciating his looks and performance. However, concern that he might whirl around while doing some wild dance move and catch her staring at him motivated her to speak.

"Excuse me," she said. He kept singing. The music was simply too loud for normal discourse. Bella cleared her throat and said, almost shouting this time, "Excuse me!"

CHAPTER 3

In one wild feat of athletics the baker jumped and twisted mid-air so when he landed he was facing her. As he was landing he called out, "Jeez, Eddie–!"

He stopped short, realizing immediately that Bella was not Eddie, or whoever he would normally expect to startle him. Remarkably, he still held the large wooden paddle in one hand as he looked her up and down, a mixture of embarrassment at being caught singing and that carnal appreciation men sometimes convey when seeing a woman for the first time. Still looking at her, he reached over and turned the volume button on an old transistor radio. The Christmas music softened.

"You're not Eddie," he said, surprise and curiosity playing in his expression.

Bella shook her head, "No, I'm not Eddie...I'm Bella."

Not quite what she thought she might say, but she was having difficulty finding words. Her normal quick wit and tendency to speak her mind failed under the curious stare of the early morning baker hired by Pits hamburger shop.

Mainly because the early morning baker hired by Pits hamburger shop was an extremely handsome guy.

With a strong jawline, full mouth, and kind eyes he could be a model or a movie star. At the very least he could be the cute cousin of a movie star.

"Bella," he grinned and nodded. Then, with a confident flirtatiousness she had always noticed in blue collar New York men, he asked, "How can I help you...Bella?"

He placed the long handle of the paddle on the floor and leaned partially against it. This stance and the Santa hat still slightly askew on his head gave him a cocky, sexy look that reminded Bella of those calendars that had a different good looking man for each month.

A Sexy Vet Brings You a Kitten in March.

A Sexy Gardener Brings You Flowers in June.

A Sexy Baker Brings You Christmas Cookies in December.

He waited patiently while she gawked at him, his gaze wandering down the buttons of her jacket where they fell on her hand. Understanding brightened his eyes and he said, "I didn't order anything, honey. You must have the wrong place."

Honey? Bella looked down and saw the forgotten wrapped breakfast sandwich in her hand. She frowned. It was one thing for a middle-aged cart vendor who was trying to cheer her up to call her 'doll', but for someone her own age to use that kind of language felt more...more...condescending.

"I'm not bringing you a sandwich," she said firmly.

"Oh, well what do you need?" He glanced at the tables in front of him, probably considering how much of his time she was taking up.

"I was hoping to speak to the owner," Bella said, finally past her speechlessness.

He looked at her more closely for a beat, then answered, "You got him."

Bella lifted her eyebrows in surprise. "You?"

His grin widened into a flirty smile. "Me."

She looked around at the basement work area. Huge stainless steel bowls, an industrial mixer, even more tables ready for more dough to be kneaded and shaped, all of it covered with a thin layer of flour, all of it speaking of a heavy workload.

He followed her gaze and looked back at her with a smirk, "Never seen an owner do any heavy lifting?"

"No, no, it's not that," she answered, though he was right in a way. She had pegged him as a worker, not a businessman.

He put the wooden paddle on the table in front of him and moved to the mixer, indicating he was continuing with his morning routine.

"Technically, I'm half an owner. Eddie's my partner." He gave her an amused look before lifting a 100-pound sack of flour onto a small table next to the mixer.

"Eddie," she repeated. He nodded. "And what's your name?" she pressed.

He pulled a Swiss Army knife out of the front pocket of his jeans and flicked it open, using the small blade to make a clean cut along the top of the bag of flour.

"My name's Mason," he answered. Without looking at her he tilted the bag and began carefully pouring flour into the mixer's bowl. "What can I do you for...Bella?" His eyes flicked up to her when he said her name. They were sea green and they smiled even as the rest of his face was all concentration on pouring the flour.

"I'm not trying to sell you anything, if that's what you're wondering."

He chuckled as flour fell into the huge mixer in soft plumps, pillows of flour puffing into the air around his hands and arms where he held the bag. "You know that's the first line any salesman, or saleslady, gives you?"

"It's not a line," she insisted. When he only chuckled again in response, she continued, "My name is Bella Velez." Still no reaction. He wrapped his arm around the center of the bag and hoisted it higher in the air to continue pouring. "I own Total." She made sure to annunciate the word with the proper Spanish pronunciation. Flour now hung in the air all around Mason, clinging to his hands as they gripped the bag and sticking to the hair on his muscled forearms. She sighed. "You know, the restaurant next door."

Mason looked at her with more interest, but didn't pause in his pouring. "Oh, yeah...I didn't know it was pronounced that way." He gave her a nod and a smile that wrinkled the corners of his eyes. "Nice to meet you."

"Nice to meet you, too," she said politely. Time to get down to business. Since he had already brought up the pronunciation of her restaurant she had the perfect opening to discuss the way their signs were clashing horribly. "I was hoping to talk to you ab–" A tickle in the back of her throat caused her to cough suddenly. Then again. She covered her mouth with her forearm, coughing into the thick wool of her coat.

Mason stopped pouring and looked at her. "You all right?"

Bella took in a deep breath, which only sucked more of the floating flour particles into her already spasming throat. She fell into a real coughing fit, eyes squeezing shut and tearing up. All conversation was lost as she fought the gag reflex at the back of her throat.

Mason straightened and put the bag of flour firmly on the table. She waved the hand holding the breakfast sandwich towards him to try and say she was fine, but the lack of air and the heat of the room made her dizzy and her wave was too large and awkward. It pushed her off balance. She swayed.

"Careful," Mason said and in one swift move he was standing next to her, his hand underneath the sandwich holding arm. Bella still coughed, the tickle in her throat refusing to allow her to regain control. "Come on," he said. "Let's get you upstairs."

He helped her up the stairs and into one of the little tables in the eating area where her coughing fit finally subsided and she focused on taking slow, careful breaths.

"Want some coffee to go with that sandwich?" he asked, his sea green eyes both amused and relieved, probably glad the strange lady who had interrupted his morning routine hadn't coughed to death in his basement.

Still unable to speak, Bella nodded. Mason got busy behind the deli counter making coffee while she tried to compose herself. Cheap paper napkins filled a shiny silver holder, similar to napkin holders in Americana diners. She pulled some of them out and used them to wipe the tears from her eyes and blow her nose.

Feeling a little more normal, Bella's gaze wandered across the other items on the table. Everything one might expect at a diner. Simple glass salt and pepper shakers, sugar and sweetener packets, a wire card holder where a small laminated menu touted 'Pits Specials' in bulbous neon font. The design filled her with dismay.

"Do you take sugar and cream?" Mason called out to her.

She had to clear her throat twice before she could answer, "No. Black, please."

"You got it," he answered and turned back to the brewing machine.

Bella looked back at the menu and read with increasing alarm.

HONEY HOLD THE PICKLE Pulled Pork Sandwich
   Nobody Loves a Pig Like We Do Ribs
   Get Your Cow On Beef Brisket

. . .

AND THE SPECIALTY DESSERT? Pits Chocolate Dump Cake

"NO...NO, NO..." Bella mumbled under her breath. She couldn't believe this. Barbecue? A pit barbecue house right next to her chic Spanish fusion restaurant? This couldn't be happening. She lifted the bottle of sauce that she had assumed was ketchup when she first saw it from across the room. Of course it wasn't. She could see for herself that it was a deep brownish red. BBQ sauce. Bella popped the lid off and held it up to her wrinkled nose.

"Here you go," Mason placed a cup of coffee in front of her and slid into the other chair at the tiny table with his own cup. It took a little doing to bend his tall frame into the space. Noticing that she was smelling the sauce, he asked, "Do you like barbecue?"

Bella paused. In normal circumstances barbecue didn't necessarily bother her, but it wasn't her favorite and she certainly didn't consider it fine dining. Especially next to her own restaurant. The smells of a pit barbecue house would clash horribly with the more nuanced fine cuisine of her beloved Total.

"I...actually...Mason." She dipped her head politely at him, ready to make her case about why he should remove his gaudy sign from the building.

"Bella," he said, his eyes twinkling merrily at her from underneath the Santa hat. Those eyes.

Bella shifted in her chair, distracted. She glanced up at his Santa hat.

Noticing the direction of her look, a question wrinkled his brow, then sudden understanding. Mason reached up and pulled the Santa hat off of his head.

"I forgot I had this on," he laughed bashfully.

Bella couldn't help but tease, "You don't wear Christmas costumes here?"

"Naw, Eddie threw it at me when he left to get supplies and I put it on as a joke." With a hint of red on his handsome cheekbones, Mason pushed the discarded Santa hat to the side of the table and focused intently on her instead. "Now, you were saying?"

Disarmed, Bella tried to find words to start her complaint again, but something outside the window caught her attention. Snow.

"It's snowing," she said simply.

Mason looked, too, delight in his voice, "Yes, it's supposed to get pretty heavy." He looked back at her with those green eyes, which were now topped with lazy spikes of sandy blonde hair. Bella couldn't think of what to say.

Outside, one of the pedestrians hurrying through the newly inclement weather caught her attention. His gait was familiar and when he got a little closer she could see it was Noah, her General Manager. Tall and heavy with a dark beard and round black rimmed glasses, his long stride always held a sense of urgency. This morning, however, with a copy of The New York Times clutched under his arm and a pensive expression he appeared even more rushed than usual.

"My rolls!" Mason exclaimed as he slammed his hands down on the table, giving her a start. His chair pushed back with a clatter as he jumped up from his seat. "Sorry, I've gotta go back downstairs."

"Of course," she said, immediately understanding that he had to take the bread out of the oven.

"I completely forgot what I was doing," Mason continued as he took quick, long steps to the door with the Lava Pit sign.

She knew how he felt.

He paused at the door and looked back at her with a genuinely appealing smile. "It was nice to meet you. Feel free to finish your coffee."

And then he was gone, leaving Bella a little flustered. She hadn't told him why she had come in the first place and now she needed to let herself out and go next door to find out what was distressing Noah.

CHAPTER 4

"Look! Just look at what it says," Noah implored as he pushed the New York Times across the counter at Bella.

Bella looked between Noah, her trusted General Manager, and Posie, her pastry chef. Behind his intellectual glasses Noah's round blue eyes were full of worry. He was practically wringing his hands. Posie, on the other hand, attempted nonchalance.

Lithe in her morning work attire of a short sleeved T-shirt with horizontal black and white stripes and a forest green smock apron, Posie busied herself pouring them all a cup of steaming coffee. With her red hair cut in a pixie style and the green apron, Bella thought Posie looked a little bit like one of Santa's elves. A bit less jolly in their present circumstances than what an elf should be, however.

"It can't be that bad, can it? We haven't even opened yet," Bella tried to push their concerns aside with common sense.

"Read it," Noah said, reaching over the counter and tapping the section containing restaurant reviews by the renowned and often persnickety critic, Nestle Bingham.

Posie caught Bella's eye right before she retreated from the full coffee cups to return the pot to its proper place. As she did, she gave Bella a little wince which could only mean that it was possible Noah was not overreacting.

With a gloomy feeling settling in, Bella turned her attention to Bingham's column.

FAILED CELEBRITY CHEF, Bella Velez, wants to bring her special brand of mediocre to the streets of New York with the opening of a new restaurant, Total. According to the press release, the name is pronounced Toe-tall. I ask you, is that at all appetizing?

I say no (pronounced noe).

Total is supposed to bring us "the delicious tastes of Bella's native Spain with her flare for fusion".

Ugh. Another fusion restaurant. Why can't these chefs simply admit they don't know what they want? Why does the public have to pay with gastrointestinal distress over their indecision? And in Velez' case, I predict that her failed TV career will add another layer of indigestion to the experience.

THERE WAS MORE, but Bella didn't want to see it. She turned the paper over so she wouldn't continue reading. She hadn't expected to be welcomed with open arms by New York's restaurant critics, but this felt especially harsh.

Dead silence sat in the room. So quiet she swore she could hear the steam rising from her coffee. She took a deep breath that sounded a little shaky.

"It's ridiculous," Noah said. "He's being hateful for no reason."

Bella gave them a brave smile. "It is his job, I guess."

Posie shook her head defiantly as she held out a bottle of

Bailey's Irish Creme. Bella nodded and Posie topped off her coffee.

"It's not his job to critique a restaurant that hasn't even opened yet. He hasn't tasted one thing off the menu," Noah added. He had switched from worried to infuriated after watching Bella read the horrible review.

"Maybe he tried a recipe off of the show?" Bella wondered.

"If he did and he didn't like it then he probably made it wrong," Posie said with a huff. She wasn't one to crumble under critique.

Neither was Bella. She took a swig of her coffee and set the tall slender mug down gently. She let the tastes of rich coffee and minty Bailey's mingle on her tongue as she looked around at the gleaming stainless steel surfaces of Total's kitchen. This was her kitchen. Her restaurant. No snarky critic was going to get her down before the doors had even opened.

She looked back at Noah and Posie who seemed to be waiting for her to make a decision. No problem. Decision made.

"Let's prove him wrong with every plate," she said.

Noah's face lit up. He loved a challenge, which was one of the reasons Bella liked him as her General Manager.

"Woo hoo!" Posie raised her fists in the air and pumped them up and down. "Lets' do it!"

Bella smiled confidently at both of them, hoping they couldn't see the hurt and anxiety that hovered just underneath. What kind of snobby food critic pre-reviewed a restaurant before they had even tasted one bite of their food? She glanced outside at the snow, which was really coming down.

"Grinch," she mumbled, imagining a pinched faced green

troll masquerading as a restaurant critic trudging through the snow.

"What?" Noah asked.

"Oh, nothing," Bella turned her attention back to them. "Okay, team. We need to come up with something big. Something glorious that this..." she pretended to check the Times for the name of the critic, though in reality his name was burned into her memory, perhaps forever. Nestle Bingham. "...this *Nestle Bingham* cannot deny is the best food and the best experience he has ever had at a restaurant."

"A party? A high profile wedding?" Noah suggested, raising his eyebrows so they lifted above his glasses with the question.

"A party!" Posie excitedly added her vote.

Bella nodded in approval. "A Christmas party?"

Noah clapped his hands together, eyes gleaming with the fun of it all. "Yes, of course...a Christmas Party."

"A beautiful Christmas Eve party...and we invite everyone who's anyone...especially this guy," Bella lifted the paper just to drop it back on the counter. "We serve him food he's only ever dreamed about," she added.

"That's it, we kill'em with kindness," Posie chimed in.

Noah leaned forward, high energy all the way. "How about this? We do a soft open a few weeks before Christmas to test out the menu a little and get the word out. Pump up interest, you know?" Noah's mind was ticking away with the details. Bella was pleased.

"Sounds great, you get started on the logistics and we..." Bella motioned to Posie. "We will get started on the menu."

"This is gonna be a blast," Posie added happily.

A loud crash interrupted them and they all looked towards the back of the kitchen. The sound seemed to come from the alley.

Another crash. Louder than the previous one.

"What is that?" Bella asked.

"Oh no," Noah said with a sigh.

"What? What's an 'oh no'?"

Noah and Posie shared a look and said in unison, "The Barbecue Boys."

"The Barbecue Boys?" Bella asked even though she was dreading the answer.

"They're really quite nice. A little rough around the edges, but in an attractive way, you know?" Noah, a connoisseur not just of fine food, but of fine men as well, explained.

Posie nodded seriously while mouthing the words 'They are HOT' to Bella.

"They're just...just a little..." Noah looked for the word.

"Loud," Posie helped him.

Another crash and Bella's felt a surge of annoyance mixed with anticipation. She knew exactly who was in the alley making such a racket.

CHAPTER 5

Sure enough, when Bella stuck her head out the back door to the alley she was greeted with the sight of Mason and another man in the process of moving what appeared to be the front section of a steam train into position against the alley wall.

Fat snowflakes stuck to the two men's heavy jackets and hats. Mason wore a regular old navy blue wool cap this time, instead of the Santa hat she had met him in, but she was still taken aback by his good looks. Somehow the extra layers of outerwear only accentuated his masculine frame and made him look that much more strong and capable.

His friend was also extremely good looking. A Black man wearing a navy blue wool cap that matched Mason's. Could this be the partner he had spoken of, Eddie?

"Eddie," Noah called out, almost in answer to her unspoken question. Noah and Posie had followed her out onto their iron grate stoop, which had a tiny awning that barely protected them from the wet snow. Noah greeted them, "Good morning, boys."

Mason and Eddie turned from their work with friendly smiles.

"Good morning," Eddie called out to them in a deep baritone voice.

Mason echoed him happily, squinting to see through the heavy snow. After the first few moments of recognition passed, Mason's eyes fell on Bella and he paused. He caught her gaze in his and his smile shifted from friendly to something a little bit warmer. The tiniest of thrills moved through Bella's heart and she smiled back at him, a slight blush kissing her cheeks.

"Hello, Bella," he said with a quick tip of his head, singling her out especially.

All eyes looked between the two of them.

"You know each other?" Posie asked.

"Well, well, well," Noah said in quiet teasing.

"How is it that you are acquainted with this beautiful woman and I am not?" Eddie teased Mason.

It was Mason's turn to dip his head bashfully and look away from her, finally noticing that everyone was watching him react to her presence.

"My apologies," Mason said with a dramatic sweeping gesture between Eddie and Bella. "Bella I would like to introduce you to my business partner and friend, Eddie Franklin. Eddie this is Bella Velez...the owner of Total."

Bella was surprised to hear him pronounce Total correctly...and that he had remembered her last name.

"Pleased to meet you," Eddie nodded in her direction.

"Nice to meet you, too," she said with a smile. Then, because there was an awkward pause and because she wanted to know, Bella asked, "What are you two doing back here...in this?" She raised her palms to the snowflakes.

"Our new smoker came in," Eddie explained.

"This is Boss Hog," Mason seemed to be introducing her to the giant steel contraption.

"Boss Hog?" Bella repeated.

"It's huge," Posie commented.

"Need some help taking it apart to get it inside?" Noah offered.

"Oh no, thanks," Mason said. "Boss Hog lives outside."

"Yeah, there's no way this guy would fit inside Pits," Eddie added. "I only wish we'd had him for the Thanksgiving turkeys we gave out. We could have done a lot more."

"Turkeys?" Bella's throat felt dry and the word came out almost as a whisper.

With an 'of course you wouldn't know, you weren't here' touch on Bella's shoulder, Posie explained, "Pits, that's the name of their place, did you see it when you came in? Anyway, Pits gave out 500 slow roasted turkey dinners on Thanksgiving. Free to the needy! Isn't that nice?"

As this information sank in, Bella's mind churned with several different thoughts at once, finally landing on the one she found most concerning.

"You're going to cook out here every day?" She glanced up and down the alley. There wasn't much to it, just doors to the buildings, each with their own iron stoop like the one she was standing on, plus a single street lamp on the end that probably did little to light up the whole area at night.

"Yes, that's the plan," Mason said. He noticed the look on her face and mistook it for concern about the cooking process. "We can get this thing cranked up hot enough to make the best barbecue you've ever tasted...unless it gets below zero. When it's below zero we'll have to stick to cooking inside."

Bella wished they would stick to cooking inside *all* of the time.

"Don't worry, we got a permit," Eddie added. "That's part

of what took so long to get it. But now that Boss Hog is here we will get him fired up in no time. Break him in before Christmas day."

"What's happening on Christmas day?" Noah was the one to ask this time.

Eddie let out a deep, pleasant chuckle, "You thought Thanksgiving was busy. We're gonna do up some Christmas hams like you've never tasted on Christmas day. Feed anyone and everyone who's hungry, no charge."

"That's the whole reason we wanted this spot for Pits," Mason told them as he motioned to Eddie and they went back to positioning Boss Hog against the alley wall. "You can't find many alleys like this in this area, and we wanted the outdoor space to cook. Barbecue tastes better when it's cooked outside, right Eddie?"

"You got that right," Eddie agreed.

"That's the Christmas spirit!" Posie said with delight.

Posie had a caring heart. More of a caring heart than Bella, she was afraid. The idea of hundreds of people lining up for a free meal on Christmas day didn't strike her as the ambiance she necessarily wanted for Total. But that was a terrible way to look at it. She could put aside her ambition for the sake of Christmas, especially because her swanky Christmas Eve party would be over by that time.

"Well, that's very nice of you both," she said generously–she hoped.

Mason gave her a big grin and again she felt a shot of something warm and fuzzy move through her heart.

"We like to give back, you know. Especially at Christmas time," he said.

"And it is beginning to look a lot like Christmas, isn't it?" Eddie added.

Then, as if they were in the middle of a Broadway musical, Eddie began to sing that very song. His baritone voice rang powerfully through the snowy alleyway. Mason joined in and they both went back to work on fitting Boss Hog into his new home.

Posie and Noah laughed at the joyful antics of the Barbecue Boys as they went back inside out of the weather. Bella tried to laugh, but she wasn't feeling terribly jolly.

Mason and Eddie both seemed like really nice people, but she didn't know if she liked their presence right next door. And worse than that she didn't know how to approach asking them to change their sign like she had planned. They were giving food away to the needy with such joyful abandon and *she* didn't want to become the neighborhood bad guy.

She scowled. How could she create the perfect ambiance for Total without becoming a Grinch like mean spirited Nestle Bingham?

On the other hand, how could she not?

Pits was encroaching on her long awaited dream of having the perfect New York eatery, and she was worried the happy-go-lucky little restaurant might ruin hers.

CHAPTER 6

Bella visited all of Total's vendors extra early the next morning, picking out thick cuts of meat, crisp vegetables, ripe fruits, creamy cheeses, aromatic herbs and ground spices, rich coffee beans, white and red wine, and fresh baked bread. Posie was busy doing the same for everything they needed to test out the baked goods for the dessert menu. The vendors would deliver all of their choices to Total where she and Posie would meet and get started. They had a lot of work to do to develop some delicious recipes worthy of the season and impressive enough to wow Nestle Bingham.

Bella didn't mind this chore at all. She adored perusing all of the choices the vendors put out for her to look at, touch, and taste. Food was her passion and she truly lost herself in the process. The sights and smells enveloped her in a cocoon of pleasure that lifted her spirits.

The vendors were friendly and knowledgeable, and though she did not know all of them very well yet, she was ready to settle into a routine and get her restaurant up and running. The baker who would be supplying them daily with baguettes and other hard rolls gave her a warm brioche to munch on as she left.

"Thank you," Bella said gratefully. She had left her apartment early and skipped breakfast.

"We'll be ready for your order," the middle-aged woman behind the counter called after her with a wave.

A bell on the door jingled as Bella pushed it open to leave. She lifted the brioche to her nose to breathe in its sweet, yeasty smell. So delicious.

Stepping out into the freezing morning air, her boots crunching on the icy sidewalk, an unbidden image of Mason in the warm basement bakery wearing his Santa hat and tank top, and singing as he baked, flashed through her mind. She smiled to herself. He had been pretty charming with his New York accent and flirtatious American attitude.

She took a big bite out of the brioche, glad she had remembered Mason. Bella wanted to remember to call her lawyer friend, Shantelle, and ask about her rights to request he move or change the Pits sign.

A twinge of regret pinched her good mood. As she munched on the brioche and made her way towards 6th Ave she was sorry her actions were very likely going to cause some negative feelings with Mason and Eddie. But she had to do the best she could for Total. It wasn't just her dream, she was responsible for keeping Noah and Posie and the others who worked for her employed.

"I'm sorry, Bella, but I don't think it would be worth it," Shantelle delivered the bad news later while Bella talked to her on her cell.

"You don't?" Bella's heart sank a little. She was standing at the wide stainless steel prep area in the kitchen perusing the various vegetables and meats that had already been delivered.

She had hoped her casual question about legally requesting that Pits move its obnoxious sign would get a thumbs up from Shantelle. Apparently not.

"No, it would be expensive and there's not really a good enough reason for a court to agree with you. I mean, it's not vulgar or anything, right?"

"No, not technically."

"Why don't you just ask them to do you a favor? You know, handle it in person instead of through a lawyer?"

Bella sighed. "Right, that would be the best way. You're right. I just thought there might be a fast and easy legal way to make it happen without too much fuss."

Shantelle's laugh came out like a snort. "Nothing legal is fast and easy."

Bella knew Shantelle was right, but she was disappointed. It would have been nice to have some vague signage law on her side when she approached Mason and Eddie with her request. Maybe it would make them feel like it wasn't her judging their taste in signs, it was simply the law.

A cold draft moved through the kitchen indicating someone had opened the front door. Noah's muffled voice followed. He had gotten in early and set up in the front while going over applications for waiters and dishwashers. Though she couldn't hear what he was saying, he was obviously greeting someone. Posie, she assumed. The kitchen door pushed open and Bella turned to find that she had assumed wrong.

"Merry Christmas!" Mason grinned at her as he stepped into the door carrying an unwieldy cardboard box. Gold and red garland flopped out of the top of the box and it clinked slightly as he placed it carefully on the stool next to her.

Surprised to see him and confused as to why he was there and what he had brought, Bella didn't know how to respond.

Mason dipped his head at her, tipping an imaginary hat, and tapped the sides of the cardboard box with both hands. "We were done decorating and had a lot of things leftover since Pits is so small. I thought maybe you might want some." When she still didn't respond, he hurried on, "Not that you don't have Christmas decorations all planned out. But since you're busy opening up..." his words trailed off and he shifted his weight from one foot to the other.

"Oh," she said, finally understanding. His visit came as a surprise, but her inability to answer him wasn't because she was shocked. Alone with him again, she was finding it difficult to think straight.

Bella's heartbeat had increased markedly at the sight of him in her kitchen. Tall and broad shouldered, a white cotton Henley with its long sleeves casually pushed up to his elbows exposing the rippled flexing of the muscles in his forearms as he managed the box, Mason's pure masculine energy got her all flustered and made it difficult for her to speak normally.

"Here, take a look and see if you like any of it," he offered, pushing the box further in her direction and stepping closer to keep it from falling off of the stool.

She swallowed and managed to answer, "Okay."

A smile brushed his lips and his eyes twinkled merrily at her. With a flutter in her stomach she leaned towards him to look into the box. He also ducked his head down to look with her and the proximity allowed her to smell his cologne, or was it cologne? A blend of fresh baked bread, old polished wood, and the snowy scent of the cold outdoors, maybe that was just the way Mason smelled all of the time.

"I think these are kinda nice," he touched an ornament, one of six carefully nestled together, which looked like bird's nests made of pine. Instead of eggs, the little pine nests were full of shining red and gold bulbs, tiny pinecones, cinnamon sticks, and a variety of gold and silver painted nuts with a silver bow on top.

"Mm-hmm," she said. The ornaments were pretty, but Bella found her eyes drawn to Mason's hand. A strong hand, long and lean, like his body, with those flexing forearms.

"Oh, and these," he lifted a strand of sleigh bells just like those she had seen at Pits.

"Aren't you using those?" she managed to ask.

"We already have some. Eddie says if I hang one more jingle bell on one more door he's quitting and moving home," Mason chuckled and the pleasant low sound of it rippled through the air and wrapped around Bella, drawing her to him.

She tried hard to focus on the ornaments, wanting to pull herself out of this mute schoolgirl reaction she was having to him, but it wasn't easy. Handsome and tall, smelling so good, standing so close, it was difficult to zero in on anything but Mason. Not even the festive Christmas decorations outshone him. The garland and ornaments, a string of star shaped lights, a glittering silver spider in the center of its own glittering silver web...

Wait. What?

She looked closer and saw that, yes, there was a large silver spider decoration inside of the box.

"Wouldn't this be for Halloween?" she asked, reaching out to touch the highest point of the silver web, her hand nearly grazing his in the process.

He shook his head and grinned. "That's the Christmas spider. For good luck."

"The Christmas spider?"

"You've never heard the Christmas spider stories? How the spider wove the blanket for baby Jesus? Or decorated the poor woman's Christmas tree?"

"No, I haven't."

"I'll have to tell them to you sometime," he said. "Or better yet, I'll get the book from my Mom. She tells them best, but they're all in books."

Surprised at the mention of his mother, she looked up into his green eyes. They were still merry, but she didn't think he was joking about going to all the fuss of getting her a Christmas spider book to read.

"I don't want you to bother your Mom," she said politely.

He chuckled again, "It's not a bother for my Mom. She loves anything to do with Christmas. And more than anything else she loves telling people about how the Polish do Christmas."

"You're Polish?"

"Yes, well my family is. You're from...?"

"I grew up in Spain. I moved here from Washington."

He nodded, but didn't say anything more. He was gazing down into her eyes and seemed to have lost his train of thought. Much like she had.

Warmth rose in Bella's cheeks and she cleared her throat, looking down shyly at the Christmas spider, not daring to look back up. Silence remained for a few long moments and she lifted her gaze back to his coyly. But her look was lost on him, because his attention was elsewhere. He was staring at the copy of the Times with Nestle Bingham's review Bella had left open on the counter, a dark furrow on his brow.

"Did that jerk review your place?" he asked.

Bella's fun and flirty mood dissipated in an instant. She glanced at the paper with a scowl and said, "Yes." Her rosy warm cheeks grew hot with the thought of it.

Mason watched her reaction knowingly. "I'm guessing it wasn't glowing?"

She shook her head, "No."

"What a..." he didn't say whatever word he'd been thinking, biting his tongue instead and looking around at her kitchen with sharp irritation. "You're not even open yet!"

"I know, right?" she scoffed indignantly, bonding with him on a whole new level.

"Well, don't you listen to a word that…" again he swallowed whatever name was on his mind. "He doesn't know what he's talking about."

"Has he reviewed your place?" she wondered.

Mason coughed out a laugh, "Pits? Naw, that foody snob wouldn't step foot in our place." He turned his focus back onto her. "And now that I know this," he jerked his head towards the newspaper, "He's not welcome."

Bella didn't know exactly how to respond to this declaration of camaraderie. Luckily, she didn't have to come up with a good answer, because Posie interrupted them.

"Hi-ho!" Posie sang out as she bumped open the swinging kitchen door with her hip. Her hands full with several different bags of baking delectables. "Or should I say Ho-Ho-H–" she stopped abruptly when she saw Mason.

"Let me give you a hand," he said and quickly went to Posie's aid, gathering all of her bags in one hand and lifting them easily onto the counter.

"Thanks," Posie said to him, but her eyes were on Bella, wide open and questioning.

Bella ignored Posie's look and set about unpacking bags and organizing the food on the table.

"Well, I'll let you two get to work," Mason said.

"Thanks," Bella responded. Then remembering, "And thanks for the decorations."

"You're welcome," he gave her another twinkle eyed grin and with a quick wave was gone.

Posie turned to face her as soon as he disappeared. "What's going on? I sense something a little flirty-flirt here."

Bella dismissed her comment with a wave of her hand and

insisted they get started on creating the menu. It wasn't until about an hour later that she realized she had missed a perfect opportunity. She could have casually brought up changing the Pits sign to something that wouldn't clash so horribly with Total's with Mason.

Instead, she had been distracted by, and nearly rendered mute, by his extreme attractive qualities—again.

CHAPTER 7

Long before the opening of her dream New York restaurant, Bella had known exactly what she wanted to serve to her patrons. The tastes of her childhood in Spain would be the base of the menu and she would add her individuality by placing touches of elegance and panache wherever made sense.

The ambiance of Total was as important as the food, this much she had learned from her friend and collaborator on their cable cooking show, Charlotte. The front of the restaurant was exactly what she had always had in mind for her own place. Shining wood floors. One exposed brick wall opposite a sleek bar with floor to ceiling mirrors. Behind the bar, shelves of glittering glass bottles and perfectly displayed stemware added the 'out on the town' vibe she wanted.

The seating area was a mix of beauty, class, and warmth. Eighteen tables dressed in thick white tablecloths with heavy silver tableware aside white on white china and black cloth napkins with silver embroidery. Crystal chandeliers hung low throughout the restaurant in bright contrast with the brick and wood while giving the whole space an almost magical quality. Finally with the large windows at the front pouring in light and giving a view of the busy street outside both night and day, Total was exactly what a person needed for a perfect dining experience in New York City.

As Noah put up the last of their rather meager Christmas decorations, Bella thought that Mason may have been right. Most of her energy and time had been going into the everyday decor of Total, and the menu of course, and she hadn't thought much about additional decorations for the holiday season. The greenery with little white lights she had purchased was quite pretty, but seemed a little sparse.

"Here," Bella produced Mason's box of bright decorations from the back closet.

"Oh, these are gorgeous!" Noah said as he reached into the box then suddenly wrinkled his large nose at the sight of the spider. "Um, isn't this the wrong holiday?"

Bella picked it up and inspected the glittery silver web. "It's supposed to be good luck."

"Then put it up right away!" Posie exclaimed as she joined them from the back office. "Because Nestle Bingham himself left a message and accepted your invitation to the soft launch next Friday."

Bella's stomach did a twirl then clenched into a tight ball of nerves. Nestle Bingham had deigned to come and eat at Total. She didn't know if she was pleased with this news or terrified. As Posie and Noah watched her for a reaction, she looked back down at the spider in her hand and decided she was terrified–but in a good way.

"I guess we better put this guy up. A good luck Christmas spider can only help, right?" she asked with a laugh. Noah and Posie shared a nervous chuckle. "We'll put him here and he can watch over everyone who comes in," Bella added as she reached up to hang Mason's Christmas spider on a small hook just behind the hostess station. She couldn't quite reach and Noah stepped in to do the actual hanging. "Thanks," she said.

"Anytime, boss," Noah gave her a friendly wink as they all stepped back and looked at the glittering spider. Bella hoped the odd decoration actually did hold some luck. They were going to need it.

They had less than two weeks to prepare for the soft open and the imminent arrival of the critic she was coming to think of as her arch enemy. Her dream restaurant was going to need every minute of that time to pull off a win.

Things moved so quickly and the days flew by so fast that Bella barely had time to think. With new kitchen staff, new wait staff, the full menu to prepare, payroll and costs to consider, there were continual fires to put out. Most were literal, but one was real when there was a small oil spill on the huge gas stove. Manuel, her new sous chef, handled that potential tragedy and everything turned out fine. At times, however, Bella felt like she was on one of those over the top reality TV shows—and she was about to be voted off.

But no, this was her life and it was crazy. It was a craziness she had craved when she was stuck doing her cooking show for the cable network. As wild as running Total was, it was a wildness that fed her soul.

On top of the kitchen whirlwind of activity, she and Noah had to work on a marketing plan. The worst thing she could imagine happening when Nestle Bingham was there, the thing she most wanted to avoid, was to have a completely empty restaurant with only the critic there to make everyone nervous. She wanted a room full of happy patrons surrounding Nestle Bingham as he ate. At the very least it would keep her and her staff occupied and they wouldn't get too nervous. Hopefully.

She and Noah visited other businesses in the area bringing gifts of tapas along with personal invitations to the soft open. Small spinach empanadas with pine nut sauce, beef chorizo croquettes, the simple yet delectable potato and egg Spanish omelet cut into tiny triangles, all delivered in black baskets with the invitation tucked inside. The baskets were a big hit with their neighbors.

She and Noah worked tirelessly to introduce Total to everyone in an eight block area. Posie extended invitations to all of her contacts in the wedding cake industry and received a positive RSVP from a well known New York socialite. Bella even invited the street vendor who had given her a breakfast sandwich on that first morning. He happily agreed to bring his wife.

As for the menu, Bella wanted to showcase the simple foods she had grown up with and add her own special twist for pizzaz.

Paella was a favorite since she was a child. She and her mother had made it several ways over the years, sometimes with chorizo, sometimes with chicken or seafood, but for Nestle, and her restaurant, Bella wanted the extra flare of something slightly more exotic. Negro Arroz, a black rice seafood paella would work nicely. Cooked in one big pan allowing the flavors to mix and the rice to form a delicious crust along the bottom, seafood paella was almost irresistible. The addition of squid ink would turn the whole dish black and lift the flavors to a unique height.

They would also serve the same tapas they had included in their gift baskets and Posie was excited to create traditional Spanish holiday candy, Turron, plus hot fried churros with an orange chocolate sauce to dip in for that evening's dessert.

"We have to work as a team," Bella instructed her new

crew in the back kitchen. With all of the talent ready to bring Total to life, she relished the opportunity to kick off her restaurant by making it clear what she expected in the kitchen. "It's going to be busy. I'm sure you expect that. It's going to get stressful, too, but I want all of us to remember that we are working towards the same goal." She smiled, unable to contain her excitement. "We are going to serve delicious food not only to critics, but to happy customers. And we're going to do it with style."

Just as she spoke these words and saw her own excitement reflected in the faces of her staff, a loud clamoring arose from the back alley. Bella closed her eyes, trying to block it out, but to no avail.

"What was that?" Manuel looked towards the back door with curiosity. They all did.

"It's nothing," Bella said with annoyance. "It's nobody."

"It's probably the guys from next door," Posie interjected. "They're a barbecue place and kind of a disaster."

"Okay," Bella said, calling the attention of her team back to her. "We don't need to worry about what the Barbecue Boys are doing."

Manuel chuckled and repeated the phrase, "Barbecue boys."

"Let's just keep focused on the tasks at hand and everything will be fine." She hoped her annoyance at Mason and Eddie wasn't seeping into her pep talk, tainting yet another special moment of her new restaurant experience.

Interruptions from Pits were a daily occurrence. Sometimes Pits customers came to the wrong front door, sometimes Pits deliveries came to the wrong back door, and all of the time the smell of barbecue roasting in the alley from five in the morning on permeated every inch of air space around Total.

Bella knew there wasn't anything she could do to get rid of them, so she chose to ignore them as much as possible. Despite all of their added chaos, she had managed to get Total into tip-top shape in only 12 days. A tremendous accomplishment in her opinion.

She wanted a warm family feeling in her restaurant as well as a sense of being a special place to eat. She wanted Total to be a restaurant where couples could come for first dates or anniversaries, where a family would return for birthday celebrations or businesses would choose for their office get togethers, where anyone and everyone who came would remember their experience as a beautiful, delectable, special occasion.

The night of the soft launch came and they were ready. Bella was pleased.

They had received several RSVPs beyond Nestle's, and she had high hopes that their first night serving customers would be a good one.

Everything was in place and looked fantastic. Noah was dressed to the nines, wearing a shiny red and black paisley vest under his black jacket. Bella, of course, was in a crisp white chef's smock and black slacks. Her hair plaited tightly into a thick braid that hung down her neck.

She mused that this was a far cry from her days doing television cooking shows with Charlotte. There they had donned full makeup and hair and new designer outfits for every shoot. But this was what she preferred. This tradition. This focus. This was about the food and the restaurant experience and this was why she had always wanted to be a chef.

Hopefully, all of this authenticity was going to help convince Nestle to retract his negative Times review and introduce Bella and Total to New York City with aplomb. A nod from a New York Time food critic would help make her kickoff Christmas Eve party a huge success.

Nestle Bingham, medium height, bald, twitchy, arrived at 7:00 pm sharp. He strode rather un-miraculously through the door and requested his table with little fanfare. So little, in fact, that both Bella and Noah almost missed his arrival.

Other guests had begun arriving at 6:30 pm and the room was already half full. Noah, busy with instructing a new waitress about serving from the bar, and Bella, busy chatting with the owner of a nearby shoe store and her wife who had accepted their tapas invitation, had turned their attention away from the entrance for only a few minutes.

The newly hired hostess, Pamela, led Nestle Bingham to his table without notifying either of them. Luckily, Bella had been sure to give Nestle's reservation the best table in the house and Pamela had followed the written instructions exactly, even though the young hostess was not aware of the importance of the critic's visit. It was Noah who saw that Nestle's name had been scratched off the reservation list.

"Did he call and cancel?" Noah asked.

Pamela, straight blonde hair framing her long face, shook her head innocently and pointed at Nestle. "No, he's seated over there. Is that right? That's where you wanted him?"

Noah gave Bella a wide eyed look of comical terror and her stomach dropped. They both turned slowly to see where, exactly, Pamela was pointing.

Though crisp in his appearance, Nestle Bingham was mediocre in the looks department. Casual, almost cheap, suit. No watch, no rings, nothing flashy on him at all. He kept a low profile as he squinted at the menu through intelligent frames sitting on a plain thin nose.

"What do we do?" Noah's anxiety was showing.

"Is everything okay?" Pamela glanced nervously between Nestle and her new bosses, afraid she had done something wrong.

Bella took a deep breath and smiled with a confidence she

did not feel. "Everything is fine. You didn't do anything wrong."

"He's a food critic," Noah explained anxiously to Pamela. The girl's eyes grew wider than his, if that was possible.

Bella looked at them both intensely. "We have nothing to be nervous about. Look at how beautiful the restaurant is tonight." She gestured to the candlelit tables, the sparkling white Christmas lights, the crystal chandeliers shimmering, the happy customers already drinking and eating their tapas as mellow Christmas jazz filled the room through their sound system. "Everything smells wonderful and looks wonderful. We've got music playing and the wine is flowing. We will serve him and he will love it and we have nothing—" she sharpened her eyes at them so they would believe what she said, "*Nothing* to worry about."

Noah visibly relaxed and nodded in agreement. "You're right."

Bella took in a deep breath and said, "I'll go introduce myself."

Before Noah could object she headed directly for Nestle Bingham's table. With every step, nerves rushed through her body, but she persisted. She had worked hard, so hard, for this restaurant and for this night. Nestle Bingham would be impressed with Total. They would change his mind so completely that he would have no choice but to write a glowing review.

He didn't look up as she approached or when she stopped and stood directly in front of him. Not until she cleared her throat did Nestle Bingham take his attention away from the menu. He blinked up at her, his eyes pale blue behind his glasses.

"Mr. Bingham?" Bella asked, hoping her voice sounded strong.

"Yes," his answer was flat and unimpressed.

"I'm Chef Bella Velez...I would like to welcome you to Tot–."

A muffled BOOM reverberated through the room causing a chorus of shouts. Silverware clattered onto dishes, a shattering of glass sounded as a shocked waitress dropped a tray of drinks, a woman screamed, and the lights went out.

CHAPTER 8

The chaos that ensued in near darkness following the explosion was complete.

Some people called out for an explanation and some gathered their things as quickly as possible to clumsily make their way to the door. A few people laughed and wondered out loud if their meals would be free. Posie's socialite guest with the tiny dog hidden in her oversized handbag, which she had been feeding tidbits of tapas all night, kept shouting, "Where are the firemen? Where are the firemen?" Frightened by her antics, her dog emitted tiny yips from the depths of her purse.

The only people who remained steely calm were Bella and, oddly, Nestle Bingham. His pale blinking eyes left her and looked around the room, taking in the scene with as much emotion as a lizard sitting on a rock. His demeanor did not change at all as he watched people hurry out the door and the staff swiftly clean up the mess of broken glass on the floor.

Noah ran to the back to see what catastrophe had occurred in the kitchen, but Bella simply stood. Her feet were stuck to the floor as she observed the mayhem around her in silence. She appeared serene on the outside, but as she tried to calm her pounding heart and decide what to do she realized she must be in shock. It wasn't until Noah burst back out of the kitchen, his round eyes reflecting consternation but not fear, that Bella shook off the surprise and was ready to take action.

"It's not us," was all he said.

She knew he meant everyone and everything in their kitchen was fine, which led to the next logical question. Where had the tremendous boom come from? Instinctively, without having to think about it for more than a beat, she knew exactly who was responsible for whatever accident had just happened.

As if on cue, Mason rushed through the front door followed closely by Eddie. Mason locked eyes with Bella and in a surprisingly commanding tone demanded to know, "Is everybody all right?"

Noah, not Bella, responded first, "Everything's fine here."

Bella thought *fine* was an exaggeration.

"The firemen are on their way," Eddie reassured them.

"Firemen? Is there a fire?" Anxiety returned to Noah's face.

"The garbage disposal blew and fried the fuse...all the fuses, actually," Eddie explained. "We'll have it back up as soon as possible. The firemen are just a precaution."

Mason, a little calmer now that he knew nobody was injured, took a moment to scan the room then looked at Bella and asked, "You're open?"

"We were open-ing," Noah said, putting heavy emphasis on the 'ing'. "A soft open kind of thing."

Bella had to grit her teeth to keep from screaming. No matter how good it would feel to blow up at Mason and release some of the pent up anger that was boiling inside of her, she knew it wouldn't serve her or Total in the long run. She didn't want to have a scene in front of the customers who remained, or Nestle Bingham, who continued to sit placidly at his table taking it all in.

Mason's eyes were full of apology. "I'm so sorry."

For a moment, an emotion other than anger flooded through Bella. Frustration so strong she wanted to cry, which was unacceptable. She grit her teeth harder and wished with all of her heart that everyone would stop looking at her.

Everyone did stop looking at her as Nestle Bingham stood to leave.

"There's no need to go, Mr. Bingham," Noah said hurriedly, even as a half-dozen customers filed out the front door, leaving long before they had been served a meal. The mood was bleak as Nestle ignored all of them and put on his coat, apparently satisfied that he'd seen enough of Total, perhaps forever.

Mason shot a look at Nestle then back to Bella, understanding written all over his face. "No, no, no, don't leave now," Mason implored. He stepped in front of Nestle Bingham, blocking the smaller man's path with his formidable height. "It's not that bad."

Sirens whined in the distance and grew louder, heading in their direction. Mason dropped his head in a defeated slump.

Nestle Bingham sniffed derisively.

Mason held up his hand like someone stopping traffic and met Nestle's blinking look firmly. "This is all my fault. It has nothing to do with Total."

Nestle looked unmoved, though he didn't try to walk around Mason.

"And we're fixing it right now," Mason said.

"Are you? It looks like you're just standing there," Bella snipped.

His eyes flicked to her and she saw that her comment had

hit its target. She felt a momentary pang of regret at hurting his feelings, but it disappeared quickly. How dare he ruin this night, this incredibly important night, with one of his ridiculous blunders at his silly little barbecue sandwich shop. His insistence that everything was going to be fine when everything most certainly was not fine did nothing but add to her anger and frustration. She knew she had ruined her chance to impress Nestle Bingham and she wasn't sure she would get another one.

Before Mason or anyone else could say anything more, she turned away from all of them to attend to the few customers who had remained through the chaos. She couldn't contain her anger and Nestle Bingham was leaving anyway. She may as well salvage her bravest patrons and try to give them a good experience.

The room was dark, but the single candles shining from each table helped. Thank goodness for those candles, though with the flashing lights from the firetruck moving rhythmically through the front windows, the ambiance was more World War II bunker than stylish dining experience.

"It'll be fixed in no time, doll," the street vendor said kindly as she checked in at his table. His name, she had learned this evening, was Jacob, and he and his wife, Sandy, were still settled in their chairs waiting for their entrees. Smiling gratefully, Bella reassured them that their meal would arrive soon and, of course, be on the house.

"Drinks on the house," Bella directed the bartender as she walked past towards the kitchen.

Posie nearly ran into her as she exited the kitchen carrying a tray stacked with turron. "I thought I would give them an extra snack while they wait." Posie peered around Bella at the dark restaurant. "Is there anybody left?"

"A few brave souls," Bella said, trying to match Posie's optimistic smile. She wasn't sure if she managed, but she silently thanked goodness for Posie and her bright, cheery personality. It helped.

She stepped into the kitchen and found her new staff doing their very best to manage the situation. Several paellas were cooking on the gas range and extra candles glowed along unused sections of stainless steel shelves. Everyone froze when she walked in, sensing her tension and uncertain about their new boss' temperament.

"Is everybody all right? Nobody's hurt?" she asked.

"No Chef, we're fine," Manuel answered for all of them.

She moved to the range and checked on the paella, it smelled wonderful. Taking a peek under the foil tent on one of the pans she saw that it looked great as well. As much of it as she could see anyway.

"Excellent job," she told them. "You're doing an excellent job and the electricity should be back soon. Thank you for all of your hard work." She felt their collective relief at her reaction, and it made her feel better, more in control.

"The dishes should be ready on time, Chef," Manuel reported with a smile.

"Thank goodness," she said under her breath. "Several of the patrons have left because..." she paused and lifted her hands into the air, letting them drop at her sides instead of trying to finish the sentence. "So it will probably be a shorter evening than we expected."

With that, Bella turned back to check on the front again. The fire truck was still parked right outside and the strobes of its lights swept through the room even though someone, probably Noah, had pulled the blinds partially down to block some of their distraction. From her perspective, the remaining patrons and staff were black silhouettes.

Squinting to see across the room, Bella spied something that made the good vibes of her visit to the kitchen slip away. Nestle Bingham's silhouette was sitting back down in his chair, which was a good thing. However, there was someone sitting with him, and it wasn't Noah.

The tall frame and wide shoulders stood out in silhouette just as they did in life. As she watched the silhouette talking and laughing with Nestle's silhouette she knew without a doubt that it was Mason enjoying a lively chat with the Time's critic. In her restaurant. In the middle of a catastrophe that he had caused.

Fuming, Bella made a beeline towards the table. She didn't know what she was going to say. She did know that she was not having that...that... *man* who baked buns in the basement of a dive called Pits infringe on her shot to make a good impression on the readers of the New York Times.

"Bella," Posie stepped in front of her, eyes twinkling with delight. "Guess what?"

Bella stopped sharply, annoyed at the interference. She bit her lip, not wanting to snap at anyone except Mason.

"I don't want to guess, Posie," she said.

Posie didn't hear the fatigue in her tone, or she chose to ignore it. She grabbed Bella by the shoulders and moved closer to her in confidence. "Do you want to know what Georgina Andreanakis wanted to know?

"Who?"

"Georgina Andreanakis," Posie flicked her eyes back and forth from Bella's confused face to the socialite with the tiny dog in her purse.

Bella glanced at the socialite. Tall, made taller by four-inch spiked heels, long unnaturally blonde hair that was straightened to within an inch of its life, large bust, also unnatural, and a nose Bella recognized as being too perfect, the woman was happily chatting to an older version of herself.

"With the dog?" Bella verified.

"Yes, with the dog. She's rich, Bella. Very rich. And she's

engaged and she's looking for a venue for her wedding. I guess it's her third and she wants to do it as fast as possible and she wanted to know if we were open to doing a wedding!" Posie's excitement was obvious.

Bella's eyes widened in surprise. "Really?"

Posie nodded enthusiastically, "She just asked me. I wanted to check with you to make sure before I agreed to something you didn't want to do."

A wedding would be good business. Good word of mouth for future business, too.

Bella nodded, "Yes, of course. We would be honored."

"We don't have anything on our calendar except for the Christmas Eve party, right?"

"Right."

"Great, I'll see what she says!" Posie bounced back to Georgina's table, excited at the possibilities. Bella, too, was flushed with the idea of another big function to get Total put on the map.

By the time she reached Nestle Bingham's table she was only fuming at about half the level she had been when she first saw Mason chatting up the critic. Mason noticed her as she approached and gave her a huge grin. She did not return it, but instead opened her mouth to say something less than generous.

"Here we go," Noah interrupted her as he arrived carrying a tray of drinks. Three in all. He placed a glass of Sauvignon Blanc in front of Nestle Bingham, a beer in front of Mason, and then he lifted the tray and offered her the remaining glass, another Sauvignon Blanc. Bella shook her head 'no'. "Is everything still good in the kitchen?" Noah asked.

She scowled at him, suspicious that he was trying to distract her from saying something she shouldn't in front of the critic.

"It's all fine. Your dinner will be here shortly," she

managed a smile at Nestle who responded by raising his thin lips on either side in a decidedly lizard-like smile.

"I'm looking forward to it," Nestle said. He motioned to Mason, "Mr. Povich has been raving about your food."

Mason grinned happily and took a big sip of his beer.

"Oh?" she feigned being flattered, knowing full well Mr. Povich had never tasted anything she had ever cooked.

"Well," Mason cleared his throat and looked at her as if she knew what he was about to say. "I told him to expect amazing things to come out of your kitchen."

She lifted one eyebrow. "You did?"

Mason nodded enthusiastically and continued, "Told him I had never tasted anything like it."

Never tasted anything at all was more like it. She ignored Mason's goofy grin. He was obviously pleased with his little charade and she didn't want to encourage him. She turned her attention back to Nestle Bingham.

"I hope you do enjoy your meal, Mr. Bingham. And I hope you will come to our Christmas-"

"Party, yes," Nestle interrupted her, giving Mason another nod. "He told me about that as well."

Bella shifted her gaze to Mason then back to Nestle. "Oh, good. He's just a mountain of information, isn't he?" She took the wine Noah was still offering her and swallowed a big gulp.

"Will you be at the party, Mr. Povich?" Nestle asked Mason.

A stab of dread shot through Bella and she tried not to pinch her nose in distaste at the idea.

"Unfortunately, I'm already booked over Christmas," Mason answered.

Temporary relief at his answer was followed by a different sense of dread when she remembered that Pits had their own plans to feed the needy on Christmas. She shook it off. There was no reason to be concerned about his event ruining hers since Total's party was planned for Christmas Eve. Plus there was the whole Peace on Earth Good Will Towards Men thing that she needed to remember.

The waiter arrived with Nestle's entree and Bella felt a surge of pride as the hot pan of seafood paella with squid ink was placed in front of him. Nestle seemed pleased, but she didn't want to stand there and watch him eat. She also thought everyone else should leave him alone to savor the dish. Noah caught her eye and understood, excusing himself politely. Mason, on the other hand, took a sip of his beer and remained seated.

Bella shifted her weight from one foot to the other, searching for a way to get rid of Mason without seeming to get rid of Mason. Suddenly it came to her.

Smiling sweetly at him, she said, "Shouldn't you be checking in with Eddie and the firemen? Make sure everything is okay?"

"I'm sure it's fine," he answered nonchalantly. "If things got out of hand those would have gone off by now." He lifted his eyes towards the small round emergency sprinklers which were placed systematically across the ceiling.

Bella's stomach dropped at the idea of the sprinklers going off. She took a controlling breath and suggested, more firmly this time, "Well, I would feel more comfortable if you would double check."

"I'm sure Eddie has it under–" Mason began, but Bella didn't give him a chance to finish.

"Humor me," she said through a set jaw.

Mason paused, finally understanding that she wanted him to leave. His eyes danced with good humor as he stood giving Nestle, then Bella, a genuine smile.

"You're right, I'll get over there and make sure."

Eyes laughing, he left Total. Bella breathed a sigh of relief, but as he passed in front of Total's front window he turned and, walking backwards, locked eyes with her.

He was still smiling and she couldn't help but give him a small smile in return. His insistent good mood was infuriating, but infectious. Just before he disappeared out of view, Mason gave her an enthusiastic two thumbs up. The move was so absurd, so unabashedly comical, Bella had to catch herself before she laughed out loud.

CHAPTER 9

Georgina Andreanakis wanted to get started right away on planning her wedding. She and her mother, the same unnatural blonde beauty who had joined her for the soft open, arrived at Total the next morning for their kickoff meeting.

"We've decided on Christmas Day," Georgina stroked the tiny head of her trembling Chihuahua in her lap with long red fingernails. "Mummy and Daddy are leaving for an extended stay in Fiji the next day so we can't wait until the New Year. And I think Christmas Day will be so romantic."

"Okay," Bella responded, only allowing her gaze to flick momentarily to Posie who stood behind Georgina and her mother. Posie's mouth had dropped open in surprise at the short timeline. Bella managed to maintain her professionalism. "That doesn't give us a lot of time, but it shouldn't be a problem."

In a way, she was excited at the challenge. A few weeks to throw Total's big opening party on Christmas Eve and then turn around the next day to host the wedding of a well connected socialite? It would be a trial by fire for her staff, and she would pay them handsomely for their time, but if they could pull it all off Total might be one of the hottest new restaurants in New York by the new year.

"I just love this building," Georgina's mother announced. "Beautiful old architecture."

"And the food has to be perfect," Georgina continued. "I like these," she picked up a cheesy mushroom croquette and popped it into her mouth. Her third. Still chewing she said, "But if I keep eating them I won't fit into my dress."

Both Georgina and her mother laughed boisterously at the comment. So loud and so long that Bella found it strange. Again she allowed herself a quick look at Posie, who appeared equally confused at their response.

"What about the cake?" Posie asked. This was her area of expertise and the part of the wedding Bella knew she was most looking forward to working on.

"We've been talking to Top Knots bakery, but we haven't decided just yet."

"I would love to show you some pictures of what we could create in house. I'll have some samples for you to taste at our next meeting if you're interested," Posie offered.

Georgina seemed delighted at the prospect of Total taking over all of her wedding preparations, which gave Posie a burst of enthusiasm. As they chatted away about tiers and fondant, something caught Bella's eye just outside the front window.

Accustomed to the normal pedestrian traffic on the sidewalk, she usually ignored the comings and goings that went on. But something not so normal was happening. Curious, but not surprised, she noted that the commotion was none other than Mason standing just to the side of Total's window.

His back was to the building, but she recognized him anyway. Not only was his particular masculine frame immediately familiar to her eye, but he was wearing his Santa hat placed slightly askew on his head. Just like when she had first laid eyes on him.

Bella narrowed her eyes as she watched him speak to someone out of her sight and laugh. Then he lifted his arm up and waved a flyer at a passing pedestrian. She contained a sigh. What was he up to?

As if reading her thoughts, Mason turned and found her watching him. Suddenly flustered, she tried to go back to her meeting, but the delight on his face at seeing her wouldn't allow her to look away.

Those laughing eyes of his had a way of drawing her in and she was forced to admit that he really pulled off the Santa hat with more than a little sex appeal. He gave her a wide smile, forcing her to smile in return and sending a warm rush through her body.

She wrinkled her brow and tilted her head slightly with the silent question, what was he doing? He pressed one of the flyers to the window so she could read it.

SPEND CHRISTMAS DAY AT PITS!
  Smoked turkey w Cornbread Stuffing
  All the Fixin's
  Free Meal for Anyone and Everyone
  Peace on Earth and Ham for All!

DREAD SHOT THROUGH BELLA, replacing the pleasant warm fuzzies. With a discreet flick of her hand she attempted to shoo him away, afraid Georgina would see the flyer and put two and two together. Georgina didn't strike Bella as the kind of woman who wanted to wade through lines of people looking for a free Christmas meal in her designer wedding gown.

"What do we have here?" Georgina cooed.

Bella closed her eyes, hoping that when she opened them Mason and his flyer would be gone. She opened them. It hadn't worked. He was still there and, even worse, he was smiling at Georgina. Thankfully he had lowered the flyer.

"Nothing," Bella waved him away again. He didn't pay any attention. Of course.

"That is a whole lot of nothing," Georgina's mother said, with more innuendo than Bella would expect from someone her age. "Hubba hubba and ho-ho-ho," she added with a girlish giggle.

Posie's eyes widened in surprise and amusement. Uncertain whether to laugh or cry, Bella turned her back to the other women and glared meaningfully at Mason. She needed him to leave.

Leaving didn't appear to be on his mind. He grinned mischievously at none other than the bride-to-be. Did he never stop with the flirting?

"If I was still single I know what I would be asking Santa to bring me for Christmas," Georgina said under her breath, but not so much under her breath that they couldn't all hear. Her mother burst into laughter and Georgina continued, "Sorry, Mr. Claus...I'm taken!" Georgina lifted her left hand and wiggled her ring finger at Mason, showing off the gigantic glittering rock that was her engagement ring.

Mason put his hand on his heart as if he'd been struck by an arrow, which only made the bride and her mother squeal with delight.

Bella scowled. Was he seriously flirting with these two?

Thankfully, whoever he was standing next to drew Mason's attention away from their meeting and he turned his back to the window. Bella couldn't wipe the scowl off of her face. Irritated and insulted she kept glancing at the back of

Mason's head out of the corner of her eye as she tried to focus her energies back on the wedding planning.

He was having animated conversations with passersby, she could tell by his gesturing and the happy expressions as they took his flyers with a smile. With the interruption over, Posie went back to discussing wedding cakes with their clients.

"I've got some pictures here of some of my previous cakes." Posie pulled out her phone to show the bride.

Bella tried to focus on the images, but couldn't shake the ugly feeling in her stomach.

Why did she let Mason get to her so much? Georgina and her mother hadn't seen his ridiculous flyer, so all was well. It didn't matter what he was doing or that he had been flirty and charming with the bleached blonde duo. Nothing he did should make any difference to her or her restaurant. But no matter how many times she told herself this, Bella couldn't brush it off.

She tried to listen as Posie held Georgina and her mother in rapt attention, but her gaze kept drifting towards the window and Mason's back. He was getting a lot of attention out on the street, and not just because he was a tall handsome man in a Santa hat. People were taking his flyers. Bella took notice of how that might be a good marketing tactic.

A thought struck her. She could do something similar for Total's Christmas Eve party.

Her mind clicked along, considering how she would distribute a flyer. Standing on the street passing them out like a hawker selling tickets to a show wasn't really Total's style. She needed a classier announcement. Something more... something like...an invitation!

Beautifully designed and specialty printed invitations sent in the mail just like an invitation to a wedding or another special, one-of-a-kind event. She smiled. She liked the idea.

Without thinking, Bella glanced at Mason's back once

more. He had inched even further away from her view and she wondered if they were done passing out flyers. It was just about time for the lunch rush. Surely he and Eddie would go inside to serve customers.

Almost as if he had heard her thoughts, Mason stepped away from the building and out of her view. For reasons she didn't quite understand, her gaze lingered on the empty space he had left behind. She thought about him in his Santa hat, which led her mind back to the moment she had first seen him in that same Santa hat, singing as he baked.

Suddenly, his face appeared again in the window. Popping in from the side like he knew she was looking for him.

Bella jumped, startled and a little embarrassed at being caught staring after him. Mason grinned and waved goodbye. Then, before he left completely, he gave her a wink. Bella's cheeks reddened. A tingle rushed over her skin.

"Ooohhh, it looks like somebody has a secret Santa admirer," Georgina's mother teased.

Bella laughed uncomfortably and turned her back to the window, wishing their planning meeting would be over sooner rather than later.

A steady stream of customers kept Bella and her team busy throughout the rest of the day. Still, at the back of her mind, she continued to imagine her special invitations and how they might impress someone like Nestle Bingham.

There was only one problem, she was not the most proficient with computer designs and she didn't have time to go to a printer and have them done. Besides, that would be one more expense she would have to take on. It would be best if she could simply print them out herself and mail them.

What could a chef with no real design skills beyond what she could create in the kitchen do? Bella knew exactly what to do and took the first opportunity she had to call her friend, Charlotte.

Combined with Bella's cooking skills, Charlotte's mad design skills had been half of the success of their cooking show. Their partnership had taken them on the crazy ride of cable TV and ended with Charlotte running a mountain Inn with the love of her life and Bella here in New York. Bella looked forward to hearing her advice.

"Is it everything you dreamed of?" Charlotte's question bubbled with curiosity on the other end of the phone.

Bella's eyes drifted around Total's tiny back office, cluttered and dark, home to all of the invoices and orders and payroll documents, it wasn't quite the glamour of the front of the house or the excitement of the kitchen.

"It's...good," she answered.

Catching her friend's hesitation, Charlotte pressed, "What's the matter?"

"Nothing's the matter...not really." Bella sighed, the challenges of the last few weeks coming to the surface.

"What's happened?"

With a friendly ear ready to listen, Bella vented all of her recent frustrations in the quiet of the tiny office. She started at the very beginning with the unhappy layout of Pits' sign next to hers, to Nestle Bingham's nasty review, to the lights going out during her soft open. She didn't hold anything back.

"Sounds like he's really gotten under your skin," Charlotte said.

"Nestle Bingham?"

"Mason, the barbecue guy."

Bella hadn't realized she had been complaining so much about Mason. "Well, he's not all bad. He brought us some Christmas decorations."

"Oh?" Christmas decorations were one of Charlotte's favorite things. "What kind?"

"I don't know, some little wreaths...and a Christmas spider."

"A Christmas spider?" Charlotte sounded surprised.

"Yes, I guess it's for good luck."

"Hmm," Charlotte didn't sound convinced. "What does he look like?"

"Oh, you know, eight legs sitting on a web. It's prettier than you'd think, actually. Silver and glittery."

Charlotte chuckled, "Not the Christmas spider. Mason. What does Mason look like?"

Bella paused and even though her friend was thousands of miles away in Colorado and couldn't see her, she tried not to blush. "What does that have to do with anything?"

Charlotte's tone sounded less concerned, more amused, "I don't know. Just curious about a man who can get you so flustered."

Bella scoffed at the idea, but she was glad she was sitting in the office away from prying eyes and ears. She wouldn't want any gossip to start up about her and Mason. Quickly, she changed the subject and explained her idea about printed invitations. Charlotte was on board.

"I can put something really beautiful together for you tomorrow," she offered. "How exciting, Bella. I'm sure it will be a party to remember."

"I wish you and Davis could come," Bella felt a little homesick for her old friend.

"We would if we didn't have a big family booked here over the holidays," Charlotte sounded equally disappointed. "It would be great to see you and see your new place." There was a meaningful pause, then Charlotte added with a giggle, "And get a look at this Mason guy."

Bella gracefully ignored the comment and turned the conversation back to the party invitations. This was a suffi-cient distraction for Charlotte and though their conversation continued for a while, there was no more mention of Mason.

When Bella finally got off the phone it was late. It had

been time well spent, she thought. She had a promise from Charlotte to email the invitations ready to print the following afternoon and all she had to do was address them and send them out. Everything was falling into place for a perfect Christmas Eve party at Total, finally.

As she walked through the nearly empty restaurant she was pleased.

The busboy, Sean, was setting up tables for the next day with clean white tablecloths and gleaming dishes. A smooth, jazzy version of White Christmas floated through the room. Noah stood at the cashier with the hostess going over the day's charges. The good luck Christmas spider sparkled above their heads.

Bella smiled. It was a beautiful image. Maybe not what everybody might find beautiful, but to her, this was heaven on earth. Even the thick snowflakes dropping past the huge picture windows at the front seemed like they had come straight out of her imagination.

Bella paused, a tiny frown puckering her mouth. It was really coming down. Big, fat, heavy flakes that had already built up on the edges of the window and frozen solid. This wasn't ideal. A little snow was great ambiance this time of year, but a heavy snow could slow down business.

She shook her head and muttered, "What next?"

CHAPTER 10

Snow filled the night and by morning the streets outside the restaurant had slowed to near silence. In New York City there was never complete silence, but the heavy snowfall had taken its toll and muffled the daily hustle.

Bella came in at her normal time, but skipped the markets. The roads and sidewalks were icy and packed with a foot and a half of snow. Her knee high boots were barely tall enough to keep the snow off of her clothes as she trudged into work. There wouldn't be many customers in the snow and there was no need to stock up on fresh goods, not until the streets were cleared up anyway.

She stopped at a mom-and-pop stationery store near her apartment. They helped her pick out an ice white card stock with flecks of silver around the edges and matching envelopes. She wanted to be ready as soon as she received Charlotte's email.

Standing at the front window of Total with her nose so close to the freezing glass that it fogged each time she breathed, she felt like a little kid on a snow day. Anticipation of her day not going quite as planned buzzed in her stomach. She lifted her eyes into the sky as far as she could see, which wasn't far because of the buildings. Thick snow continued to fall, swirling slowly down and down until it added itself to the mounds covering the street outside.

"Not supposed to stop until late this afternoon," Noah said, handing her a hot mug of coffee. He stood next to her taking careful sips from his own steaming drink and pondered the weather.

"Do you think this will bring people in or keep them away?" she asked.

Noah grunted. She knew what he was thinking. Business had been slow thus far, not enough people knew they were open. It was unlikely this snowstorm would be the thing that changed that.

She sighed. "May as well call everyone and tell them not to come in. If we need them we'll let them know."

They busied themselves as best they could. Noah went through paperwork and paid bills. Bella decided to try out some different flavors in the kitchen. There was some salmon that should be used that day so she got creative and tried five different spice mixtures for blackening. Three of them turned out okay. One was delicious. But one was a disaster, which she threw out immediately.

When she was in the back alley emptying the contents of her pan into the dumpster, she noticed that Boss Hog sat cold and unused. Normally, Mason and Eddie had so much barbecue in that monstrosity that the scent of cooking meat steamed out of it all day long, filling the surrounding area with its smoky smell. Pits must be taking a snow day as well.

By two o'clock Bella sent Noah home. There was no sense in both of them wandering around the restaurant looking for something to do.

"I can help you address these," Noah offered, holding up the envelopes from the stationery store.

"I think I can handle that on my own."

"Well, all right," Noah pushed his glasses up on his nose and Bella could tell he didn't like the idea of leaving her there alone.

"I'm fine," she insisted.

"It's just so dead. What if someone decides to rob the place?"

Bella laughed. "I don't think I need to worry about anybody coming in here except maybe an abominable snowman." Noah laughed reluctantly. "Here," she said, taking the envelopes from him and a pen. "I'll do all of these at the front table so I can see if anyone comes in."

Settled in at the table directly facing the street with a pile of envelopes, a glass of wine, and a promise that she would keep the front door locked unless 'actual paying guests' arrived, Bella watched Noah make his way through the snow in the direction of his apartment. It was a cozy feeling to be in her restaurant in the middle of the afternoon with nobody around.

"Okay, Mr. Bingham," she said out loud. "Let's get yours done first."

Using her best handwriting, Bella addressed the first envelope to Mr. Nestle Bingham. It looked quite pretty on the fine stationery. She was glad she had splurged.

The snow was beginning to taper off, the buildup outside looked like it could be more than three feet deep. Staring out the window at the mess, Bella started to wonder when she should consider going home, when two familiar figures crossed the street toward her building.

Mason and Eddie jogged carefully through the mucky snow caused by cars braving the drive. They both wore sweat pants under their jackets, like they had been working out together.

Eddie said something and they looked in her direction, almost as if they had been talking about her. When they saw her watching them from the window Bella looked down quickly at her envelopes, but glanced up just as quickly. Mason waved and she waved back as casually as someone who has been caught staring can wave.

Charlotte's teasing came back to her and she suppressed a bashful smile. She peered at his and Eddie's figures as they disappeared past the edge of her window, going back into Pits. They were both good looking men. She was sure Charlotte would agree.

After she finished addressing all of the envelopes, Bella checked her phone for the umpteenth time to see if Charlotte's email had come through yet. Nothing. Pressing the volume button she turned it all the way up so she wouldn't miss the notification then scrolled through weather predictions for the city over the next few days. It looked like the snow was clearing out over the afternoon, leaving a big clean up behind.

A *knock, knock, knock* sounded on the window pane.

Bella let out a startled yelp, and jumped in her chair at the sight of Mason grinning at her from the sidewalk.

"Ho ho ho!" His voice was muffled by the frosty glass.

He motioned at Total's entrance and jogged towards the door, his breath clouding in the freezing air. Bella met him there, but wasn't fast enough to unlock the deadbolt before he tried the doorknob. The knob wiggled setting off the sleigh bells hanging off of it, but the door didn't budge.

"Hang on," she said as she turned the deadbolt and pulled the door open.

"I'm sorry, you're closed?" Mason eyed the empty tables behind her.

"Yes and no," Bella backed up letting him in and out of the cold. "No customers."

"Yeah, it's been the same for us today. We closed up and hit the gym."

"I saw that," Bella said before realizing that might sound a little like she was watching his every move. To keep him from noticing, she threw out a random question, "What gym do you go to?"

"Mo's," he said, stamping the snow off of his feet. She noticed he had changed into jeans.

"Oh? I haven't heard of that one."

"It's a boxing gym. That's all they do."

Boxing. That would explain his physique.

"You box?" She couldn't help but sound impressed.

He shrugged. "Not in the ring. Not anymore. But the workout is good exercise." His eyes twinkled a little as he added, "You should try it."

"Me? Boxing?"

"Yeah, it's good for stress."

At his insinuation that she was stressed, her shoulders tightened. He might have a point.

An awkward silence followed, leaving Bella long enough to think about the fact that she and Mason were absolutely alone. Snow on his hat and jacket melted in the warmth of the quiet restaurant and she noticed that the hair peeking out from underneath his hat was wet.

Mason lifted his eyes to the Christmas spider and smiled, "I see you found him a home."

"Oh, yes. He's quite a conversation starter."

He chuckled then let his eyes roam over the empty tables, landing on her pile of hand addressed envelopes.

"Getting some paperwork done?" he asked.

"Yes, well, invitations actually. To our Christmas party."

Mason nodded and rocked back on his heels, staring at

the floor between them. He seemed to be waiting for something, but Bella couldn't imagine what.

He cleared his throat. "I was wondering if...since you're not busy and we're definitely not busy..." his head still bent towards the floor, he raised his eyes to look at her. "I was wondering if you'd like to go window shopping with me."

She paused, her general irritation with him pausing as well. Heat rushed to her cheeks, but she couldn't look away from his eyes. Normally twinkling with fun, they were a bit bashful, a bit hopeful, and a bit daring, as he waited for her to answer.

She started to speak, but instead of words, a sudden laugh escaped her lips and she looked down at the floor between them where Mason had been staring just moments before.

Emboldened by her non-refusal, Mason began a convincing argument, "It's not every night that's gonna be this slow, you know. You may not have another chance to get out and see the sights. And everything's so beautiful with the snow."

She looked up at him, her stomach buzzing with the compliment of being asked out. When their eyes met his body bent towards her, a quiet plea for her to consider his request. Through the smell of melted snow and slush from outside Bella caught his unique scent, polished wood and fresh baked bread. A smile played on her lips.

He cocked his head and gave her a sad smile exaggerating his let down. He tried one more gimmick, "*And* it's Christmas time. You can't turn a guy down at Christmas time."

She laughed again, looking coyly to the side where she caught sight of her pile of envelopes. "I have some work to get done...unfortunately." Bella was caught off guard by her own disappointment.

"Aw, no!" His knees bent as if he had just rolled a losing pair of dice. Mason followed her gaze and saw the envelopes.

"If I helped you stuff some envelopes would you take off and go with me?" He looked back at her with hope.

"Actually, I'm waiting for a—" She was interrupted by the blaring double ding of her phone on full volume telling her that she had just received an email and a text. "...an email." Charlotte had sent the design as promised.

Before she knew what was happening, Bella found herself standing at the envelope table explaining her plans to Mason as he admired her penmanship. She eagerly looked at Charlotte's email as she talked, immediately impressed with the invitations. The email specified that Charlotte had left the date, time, and address blank for Bella to fill out for accuracy.

"What do you think?" Bella turned her phone so Mason could see the image of the invitations. Elegant lines created intricate snowflakes along the edges and the top of the invitation. Scrolling cursive made up the text in the center. Bella couldn't wait to see how it looked printed on the silver flecked paper.

Mason let out a low, appreciative whistle. "Nice. Are you printing them here?"

"Yes, in the back."

"My offer stands. I'll help you out...if you want." Bella hesitated, but only for an instant before she nodded excitedly. Happy to oblige, Mason shed his jacket and hat, hung them on the back of the chair, then gathered up the envelopes. "Lead the way."

Bent over the small laptop and printer that served all of Total's computer needs, they worked together to get the invitations done. While Bella logged in to her computer and downloaded the invitation file, Mason unwrapped the silvery white card stock.

The tiny office was full of Mason's presence. Sitting just behind her and to the right, he stretched his long legs to the side in a polite attempt to give her more room. It didn't make much difference, the sensation of him being so close to her, watching her from behind, made her feel animated and giggly.

"Who made it for you?" he asked, nodding towards the image of the invitation on her laptop.

"My friend, Charlotte. She's great with design. We used to work together on our TV show."

There was a pause before he asked, "You had a TV show?"

Bella laughed at his surprise. Not that she expected everyone to recognize her from her cooking show, but she had assumed Mason knew. She looked back over her shoulder at him and saw he was sincerely curious and maybe more than a little impressed.

Shrugging it off, she turned back to the computer. "Just a little cooking show. It didn't work out." Her fingers clicked busily on the keyboard, typing in Total's address in the space provided.

"So this party's gonna be a big deal." It was a statement more than a question as Mason mulled over her previously unknown celebrity status.

"Maybe...I hope so." And to move past any awkwardness over her television experience, she added, "Yours will be a big deal, too."

"My party?"

"Yes, the Christmas dinner you're doing."

"Oh, right. Yes, that should be...busy," he chuckled at the thought. A deep, rumbling sound that affected Bella more than usual in this small space.

Every time he spoke the sound of his voice vibrated and tickled the back of her neck. The sensation was pleasant, but distracting, and she fat fingered the month December, typing *Decenver* instead.

"We've scheduled a wedding for that day," she said, carefully deleting the incorrect letters.

"Christmas Day? That'll be huge."

She nodded, wishing she could ignore the way he was leaning casually in his chair, watching her every move and smelling so good.

"It's that woman and her mother that were here the other day. You saw them...when you were passing out flyers." Bella winced at her own sentence. Why she felt the need to make sure Mason knew Georgina was getting married, she wasn't sure.

"Oh, her," he chuckled again. "The one with the huge ring."

"Yes, her," Bella tried to squelch the tiny spark of jealousy in her chest. She was being ridiculous. She retyped the date and time. *December 25th, 6:00pm to 11:00pm.*

She printed the invitations out on the silver flecked paper and folded them in half so they would fit into the envelopes. As she folded each one, Mason dutifully stuffed it into an envelope and sealed it. In just a few minutes there was a pristine stack of invitations ready to mail.

"Is that all?" Mason had run out of envelopes even though there were two printed invitations remaining.

"That's all for now."

"Should we take them to the mailbox?"

"Noah's going to do that in the morning for me."

Mason nodded, looking around the little office as if taking stock. When he looked back at her, his sandy blonde hair charmingly unruly since he'd removed his winter hat, his eyes were full of their usual fun.

He grinned, "Now that your work is done, are you ready for some Christmas cheer?"

CHAPTER 11

By the time they reached 5th Avenue and stood in front of Saks, the snow had all but stopped. It left behind a sharp cold and several inches of already dirty downtrodden drifts. Snow so cold it had the consistency of sand and ground under their feet instead of melting into ice.

Though the night air bit her nose, Bella marveled at how warm she felt. Mason's gloved hand held hers firmly, partly for warmth, partly to guide her along through the crowds that had gathered on this famous street, but mostly, she hoped, because he wanted to hold her hand.

"This is outstanding," Mason declared.

Bella agreed.

Saks' theme for the holiday was The Nutcracker. Each window depicted a different scene from the famous ballet and the displays were as lavish and awe inspiring as she had always thought they would be. Though she had spent a lot of time in New York City, Bella had never been in the city during Christmas.

Bloomingdale's, Bergdorf's, all of the window decorations

along 5th Avenue were beautiful, but something about The Nutcracker scenes were especially gorgeous. They were at once familiar and breathtakingly brand new. Each had been reimagined with such care and detail that Bella felt like a little girl gawking at them from the street outside.

They paused in front of the Sugar Plum Fairy scene and did not move for a few minutes. Mason was just as taken with the windows as she was, which Bella liked. It wasn't every man who took the time to pause and delight in pure beauty.

Their time together strolling in the icy cold night had been surprisingly fun. They had chatted about the different Christmas traditions of their families. His were very Polish, hers came from a childhood in Spain. They had paused and admired all of the lovely window decorations and other outside light displays. He carefully led her around and through various obstacles which included other pedestrians and dangerously deep sections of snow. She liked the way he brought her close to him and placed his hand on her back for extra protection.

The Sugar Plum Fairy was the longest they had stayed in one place during their adventure and Bella took a moment to glance up at him while he was distracted by the window. Struck once again by how tall and handsome he was, a swell of attraction shimmered through her heart, warming her from the inside out.

Mason looked down and smiled, a smile that started in his eyes. He squeezed her hand gently and everyone else on the street disappeared. All Bella could see was the shine in his eyes that sparkled like the Sugar Plum Fairy scene.

She had grown used to him holding her hand and his body moving closely with hers as they walked. So much so that she barely noticed he was drawing her closer to him, his face tilting down towards hers, his gaze dropping from her eyes to her lips.

"I..." she started to say something though she didn't have any idea what words were going to come out of her mouth.

Mason paused, his face so close to hers that his breath warmed her cheeks. He lifted his gaze back up to hers and the look boggled Bella's speech pattern.

"Bella...I–" he started to speak, but was interrupted by Tchaikovsky's famous tune, The Dance of the Sugar Plum Fairy, resounding from unseen speakers on the Saks Fifth Avenue building.

The music was so sudden and so loud it was startling not only to her and Mason, but to all of the other gawking spectators on the sidewalk. A few shouts of surprise and delight came from the crowd followed by cheers. The side of the building changed from stone and brick to the shining spectacle of a Sugar Plum castle.

"The light show," Mason announced, with more than a little excitement.

"Right," Bella realized she'd been holding her breath and exhaled. "The light show."

Mason swung her hand to the music and raised his other hand, conducting with his forefinger. Bella laughed at his boyish enthusiasm.

He hummed along with the song. Not too loud, just loud enough that she and maybe the people closest to them could hear. Everybody's attention was drawn to the light display going on over their heads.

"Come on," Mason said. "We can see it better over here."

He pulled her hand and she followed. Bella let him lead her quickly around the crowd barriers blocking direct access to the street to the crosswalk. The crosswalk light blinked a warning that they had less than a few seconds. Ignoring the warning sign, he hurried them across the street and into the crowd on the other side who were all staring up at the light show. When she started to breathlessly protest being yanked around in such a hurry, Mason took her by the shoulders and turned her towards the Saks Fifth Avenue building.

"Look at that," he said, pride and passion in his voice.

The music played loud enough to hear over the nearby traffic noise and the buzz of the excited crowd. A castle made of light blinked and shimmered in rhythm with the tune, ebbing and flowing back and forth across the solid surface of the building, creating the optical illusion that the castle was lifting off the ground and floating into the air.

Bella shivered. Not because of the cold, but because of the beauty and excitement of it all.

"You're cold," Mason said. She almost corrected him, but he wrapped his long arms around her shoulders from behind in an attempt to keep her warm. Even through the layers of clothes, jackets, and scarves, Bella could feel his strength. She didn't mind his misinterpretation of her shivering, especially when he started humming the tune again and the vibration of his singing moved through her body. On top of the physical sensation his singing gave her, it sounded wonderful as well. He had a great voice.

"You have a good singing voice," she said.

The humming stopped. "You think?"

"I do."

Encouraged by her compliment, Mason's humming grew louder and he swayed her gently from side to side with the music. Her body responded to his, following his lead fluidly, sinking into him. Gently, so gently she thought for a moment she may be imagining it, Mason pulled her even closer, shifting his arms further down her body so there was no way she could move away from him.

Not that she wanted to.

She could have stayed that way forever. Warm and safe, watching the beautiful lights, the energy of the season all around them. It was like a dream. Surprising in its appearance, yet touching something deep inside of her heart. So complete was her response to the feel of him holding her and the sound of his voice humming in her ear that she knew it must mean something...maybe something big.

Maybe she had been alone too long. Maybe she had been focusing too much on her business and success in her career. Maybe what she wanted, needed, was a man like Mason to whisk her away into romance.

The light show did not last forever, unfortunately. It was over after a few minutes and it seemed like they had come to the end of a grand moment. Mason turned her back around to face him, the giant Christmas tree of Rockefeller Center in the distance behind him created a dim halo around his head as she gazed up into his eyes.

"You're cold," he said. Not asking, just stating it as fact. "Want to get some coffee?"

Not quite the romantic moment Bella had been anticipating, but coffee did sound good.

Bella swallowed, finding it hard to respond after her recent surge of romantic attraction to him. She managed to croak out, "Sure."

They walked to a nearby coffee shop. Warmed by the bodies of the people crowded inside, the aroma of fresh brewed coffee and the baking of sweet goodies, the little shop buzzed with activity. Bella soaked it in, relishing the cozy vibe.

"Thanks for coming with me," Mason said.

They sat at a tiny bistro table he had snagged in a dark corner of the coffee shop, out of the way of the draft from the almost continuously opening and closing door. He had taken off his hat and the familiar lazy spikes of his hair were in complete disarray. Bella was sure she, too, suffered from hat hair, but something about being less put together than normal added another layer of intimacy to the moment.

"I enjoyed it. Do you come every Christmas holiday?"

"I used to. My Mom always brought us when we were kids. We would come here and then go ice skating in Bryant park. They have a big Winter Wonderland shopping thing they do there. We could never afford to buy anything, but it was fun to go walk through it all."

"And who is we, exactly?"

"Me and my little sister."

Bella listened as she broke off a chunk of the gooey peppermint chocolate cookie Mason had brought back from the counter along with their coffee. Bella loved peppermint and chocolate at Christmas time.

"Yeah, it was something we could do at Christmas that didn't cost anything. After my Dad died money was kinda tight."

A twinge of sympathy stung her heart. "I'm sorry. How old were you when he passed away?"

Mason's gaze dropped to the table. "Seven...Mavis was four."

"Mavis is your sister?"

"Yeah," he tapped the edge of their shared cookie plate thoughtfully.

"My Dad died when I was 10," Bella said. She didn't normally discuss details of her family life with near strangers, but it felt like the right thing to say. For some reason she wanted Mason to know.

Mason looked up at her through the shag of messy hair that had flopped over his brow. The normal twinkle of fun in his eyes was gone, replaced by something far deeper. Sea green like always, but darker and shining with an intensity that made it impossible for Bella to look away.

Not that she wanted to. The sensation was strange. Connection.

Locked into the pain in his eyes, which mirrored the pain

in her own. Not only pain. Bella saw something else in the deeper green of Mason's eyes. She saw longing. A longing for comfort, for home, for family. It was as plain to her as if he had spoken the words out loud and it held her there, suspended in this warm cozy space, surrounded by the world, yet completely lost in each other.

Bella forgot everything. She forgot her cold toes, the snow outside that had closed Total for the evening, the huge upcoming events she had to plan, Nestle Bingham's bad review, the invitations waiting to be mailed, the way Mason's barbecue restaurant drove her a little nuts. There was only his eyes, the square line of his jaw, the way his mouth held a hint of a smile all the time, his broad shoulders leaning towards her dwarfing the tiny coffee shop table, and how close his strong, capable hands were to the peppermint chocolate cookie...which was extremely close to her fingertips.

"I'm sorry that happened to you," Mason said, his voice throaty, quiet.

Bella dropped her eyes to his hands. Her heart jumped into her throat. She wasn't equipped for this. She wasn't ready to start crying in front of him.

"How did you deal with it?" she asked, hoping she could focus on his childhood pain instead of hers.

He lifted one shoulder and dropped it then scanned the nearby tables without really seeing them. "At first I caused my Mom a lot of trouble, fought a lot at school, you know. When I got older I took up boxing like my Dad. And eventually I joined the army."

The twinge of sympathy again. Imagining Mason as a messy haired little boy fighting with the other kids in the playground while he tried to deal with his father's death broke her heart.

"What about you?" he asked.

"Oh, well I...I helped my Mom. We cooked."

His face softened and he smiled. "Cooked. Of course."

Christmas music played as the other patrons of the coffee shop chatted happily. The sounds returned around their little bubble of intimacy and though Bella wasn't quite as lost in his eyes as she had been moments before, she felt a new level of comfort with Mason. As if they had known each other for longer than just a few short weeks.

Harry Connick Jr's voice crooned his rendition of "What Are You Doing New Year's Eve?". The swanky piano and saxophone music combined with his smooth voice was a perfect blend. Mason seemed to notice the song at the same time she did and moved his torso ever so slightly back and forth to the music.

The twinkle returned to his eyes and he leaned closer to her and sang along, just loud enough for her to hear, "Ah, but in case I stand one little chance. Here comes the jackpot question in advance. What are you doing New Year's Eve?"

Bella giggled, not sure if he really meant it or if he was just singing the words to the song. "And when did you learn to sing?" she asked.

"That was my Mom. She made me sing in church to try to counter my juvenile delinquency," he chuckled.

"You do have a great voice. It sounds like you've had more training than that."

Cheeks turning red, he admitted, "I sang in the Army, too. Infantry band."

"Really?"

He nodded and broke a piece of cookie off. "That's where Eddie and I met. Then I convinced him to box too, to kind of counter the whole singing thing." He wiggled his eyebrows at her and popped the cookie into his mouth.

"You don't sing in the church choir anymore?" she teased. He chewed the cookie heartily, trying to fight the reddening of his cheeks again. She laughed out loud. "You still sing in the church choir?"

Mason swallowed and made a show of wiping his mouth with his napkin before answering, "It's for my Mom. She gets a kick out of it."

"That's sweet," she said.

"Man," Mason took a swig of his coffee. "That cookie is sweet."

He was trying to change the subject and Bella let him. She didn't want to embarrass a man who was willing to sing in the church choir for his mother.

"Yes, it is. It's delicious, but I don't think I can eat any more."

Mason's face fell, "You haven't eaten dinner, have you?" Bella shook her head 'no'. He looked her up and down as if she was about to keel over and fall off of her chair. "I should have taken you to get real food."

"It's okay—"

"No, I'm sorry. I got all caught up wanting to bring you to see the light show."

"I'm fine, really."

"I'm usually better at this."

"Better at what?" Bella couldn't imagine having a better time than what she had experienced the last few hours with Mason.

"Better at feeding people."

"Oh," she laughed a little. Of course, he was a feeder.

"Will you let me make it up to you?"

Bella smiled. In fact, she couldn't stop smiling long enough to answer.

"Let me take you out for something to eat," Mason suggested.

"Now?"

"Now, tomorrow, whenever you want."

Nerves fluttered in her stomach. She was gripping her hands together on the table, but didn't realize it until Mason reached over and covered them both with just one of his.

Clenching her jaw to try to keep it from shaking as she spoke, Bella had the feeling she was answering a much larger question than the one he had asked when she responded, "Yes, I would like that."

CHAPTER 12

"Someone woke up on the right side of the bed," Posie said as she melted sugar and water in a saucepan on the stove. She was in the middle of preparing flan, but kept giving Bella sly sideways glances as she stirred.

The comment pulled Bella out of a wild scenario she was imagining that included her and Mason taking a vacation to the Mediterranean so he could meet her mother.

"What?" Bella asked, coming back to reality and the bowl of cheese filling in front of her. She was mixing it up for an updated mushroom cilantro croquette she was thinking about changing on the menu.

"You were humming," Posie said, amused.

"I was?"

"Mm-hmm," Posie continued stirring. "Christmas Carols."

Bella giggled, "I didn't realize."

"I figured. So...are you going to tell me why you're walking around on a cloud this morning?"

"Who's walking around on a cloud?" Noah bustled into the room with his leather attache case hanging from his shoulder and a stack of mail and small boxes in his gloved hands.

"Bella," Posie volunteered.

Noah looked at Bella excitedly, "And what are you so tickled about? The party?"

Bella had all but forgotten about the Christmas Eve Party, or at least put it at the back of her mind. Ever since Mason walked her to her door last night and they said goodnight she had not been able to stop thinking about him.

She had fumbled her apartment key so badly he reached around her and put his hand over hers, saying, "Let me get that."

Confidence permeated everything he did, which at once made her feel both safe and excited. She had been sure he was going to kiss her goodnight, but he didn't, and that turned out to be even more appealing. Leaning on her front door frame, his arm passing just by her ear, his elbow bent, Mason had bent down towards her and Bella lifted her mouth towards his instinctively.

Inches away from a first kiss, he allowed his eyes to linger on her hair then her cheek then her lips before looking up into her eyes and softly saying, "Thank you for tonight, Bella," then pulling away and walking backwards down the street, never looking away from her.

Her knees had wobbled all the way into her apartment. When she shut the door she leaned back against it for support and closed her eyes, her heart still beating wildly in her chest.

"I mailed all of the invitations," Noah said.

Bella blinked at him, taking a second to remember where she was...in Total's kitchen...making mushroom cilantro filling.

"Oh, you got them done?" Posie asked excitedly as she inspected the near boiling sugar in her pan.

"I did," Bella said, remembering Mason sitting behind her as she worked at the desk then helping her stuff and seal envelopes. Butterflies flitted through her stomach. "There are a few extras on the desk if you want to look at them," she told Posie. Turning to Noah she continued, "Thank you for mailing those." Noah was giving her an odd look. She hesitated, blushed, then asked, "What?"

Noah's round eyes were full of fun, "Well, well, well, Miss Velez...is something different about you?"

"Nothing's different," Bella tried to look like she hadn't been walking in a dream world all morning.

Noah shared a doubtful look with Posie then grinned mischievously at Bella, "You're smiling."

"And humming," Posie added as she poured the caramelized sugar into the first of dozens of white ramekins.

"Smiling and humming, hmm, what's putting you in such a good mood?" Noah asked.

"Nothing in particular. I'm just glad the storm is over and more customers will be coming in today."

"That is a good thing," Noah agreed. "And I brought this!" He lifted a CD case from his bag and wiggled it at them. The image on the CD was a Christmas wreath with the title 'Christmas Classics' emblazoned across the front.

"A CD, really?" Posie teased.

"Hey, you can't find some of these songs on streaming. They're too..." he looked for the word.

"Old?" Posie laughed.

"Classic!" Noah declared, pretending to be insulted.

"Speaking of customers, I have a few emails from Georgina I need to read through for our next wedding planning session." Bella tore a piece of plastic wrap from the giant roll at the end of the counter, covered her cheese filling, then stuck the bowl into the industrial refrigerator. "I'll take that and put it in the player in the office," she reached for the CD.

"Right," Noah chuckled, his eyes squinting with faux suspicion. "An excellent excuse to escape questioning."

"Thank you," Bella called over her shoulder as she left the kitchen, CD in hand.

Alone in the small office she remained awash with the pleasure of her and Mason's secret date. Bella hummed to herself as she put the CD in their antiquated stereo system and pushed the play button. Jimmy Durante's unmistakeable version of Frosty the Snowman from the original animated movie piped through the still empty restaurant.

She was delighted. Everything delighted her this morning. What she wanted to do was dance, but she satisfied the urge by tapping her foot and singing along with the song as she sat at the desk and reviewed Georgina's emails.

Fifteen minutes later Posie ducked into the office, sketchbook in hand. "I have some ideas for the wedding cake I want to show you."

Bella twirled the office chair around to face Posie, "Ooooh, how fun!"

Posie giggled as she plopped down in the chair Mason had sat in the night before, smiling down at her drawings. "The spirit of Christmas must have bit you in the behind."

Bella laughed. "Is that how that works?"

Posie shrugged, "Something like that. Are these the invitations?" She picked up the two extra invitations that Bella had left on the desk.

Bella nodded happily while Burl Ives started singing Have a Holly Jolly Christmas over the speaker system.

"Do you like them?" she asked.

"They're gorgeous," Posie gasped. "So elegant, but still simple, you know?"

"Yes, Charlie's a genius at design." Bella picked up the sketchpad with the wedding cake diagrams, amazed at Posie's artistry while Posie admired the invitations.

"Um...what's this?" Posie's brows furrowed in concern.

"What's what?"

Burl Ives crooned for them to have a Holly Jolly Christmas by Golly, but Bella wasn't listening anymore. She didn't like Posie's expression. She looked shocked and dismayed.

"This!" Posie jabbed her forefinger at the center of the invitation. She looked up with round, horrified eyes. "Bella, is this what you printed on all of the invitations?!"

CHAPTER 13

Bella stared in disbelief at the invitation Posie had turned for her to see.

"December 25th..." she said numbly.

"December 25th," Posie annunciated the number, eyes still wide.

"December 25th is Christmas Day," Bella said. As the words came out of her mouth her voice echoed in her own ears as if she was standing outside of her body listening.

Posie nodded emphatically and flipped the invitation back to double check it before giving it to Bella who had reached out her hand.

Bella read the words printed on the invitation several times. Burl Ives' Holly Jolly lyrics growing louder and louder as her mistake sank in.

You are cordially invited to a Total Christmas
December 25th, 6:00pm to 11:00pm

. . .

"It says December 25th not December 24th," Posie continued to state the obvious. "Are these two mistakes? Did you print a different version to go in the mail?" She sounded hopeful.

Bella knew she had no reason to be. "I put December 25th on the invitations to the party." It was her turn to state the obvious. But she had to, because it didn't seem real. How could she possibly have made such a massive mistake?

"The wedding is on December 25th," Posie reminded her. "I thought the party was going to be on Christmas Eve, the 24th."

Again. So obvious.

"It is...it was..." Bella's voice was almost a whisper. The reality of what she'd done sank into the pit of her stomach.

Posie picked up the second extra invitation and stared at it with such intensity Bella thought she may be trying to change the typo via mental telepathy.

Holly Jolly Christmas ended, leaving a deafening pause for a few moments where Bella and Posie each stared at the invitations they clutched with growing alarm.

Georgina's wedding was at 6:00pm on Christmas Day. Their Christmas Grand Opening Party was at 6:00pm the same day. There was no way they could do both.

The happy tinkling of another oldies Christmas carol began and Dean Martin's gravely voice sang about the weather outside being frightful. Bella and Posie remained still, the full weight of their dilemma bearing down on them. When the chorus began Noah danced into the office, singing along with the lyrics.

"Let it snow, let it snow, let it sn—" he stopped abruptly at the sight of their faces. "What's the matter?"

What followed was a blizzard of despair. Bella and Posie both explaining in rapidly escalating tones how Bella had accidentally printed all of the invitations to the party with the same date and time as Georgina's wedding.

Noah's face paled, his big blue eyes large and anxious behind his glasses. "The invitations that I put in the mail?"

Bella and Posie both nodded emphatically.

"Can you get them back?" Posie asked, a glimmer of hope in her voice.

Noah sank against the doorframe, deflated. "I took them to the post office...inside...directly into the outgoing mail slot."

Bella moaned and buried her face into her hands. Noah and Posie made soothing sounds, but they were lost on her. Her stomach roiled and she thought she might be sick. Ugly words popped into her head.

Nothing ever worked out. Her life was messy, sloppy, disappointing, full of missed deadlines and epic mistakes.

The only true success he had ever had had been her cable cooking show with Charlotte, and that had all been based on a lie. She had gotten so sick on their audition day she had insisted Charlotte take her place as the chef and because of that decision was doomed to work as Charlotte's assistant forever. Out of the spotlight and unnoticed, she never received any credit for the recipes she developed on the show.

In her next big mess up Bella had missed the flight to Colorado, which ultimately exposed her and Charlotte as frauds. All had turned out okay for Charlotte, as she had never wanted to be a celebrity chef to begin with, but cooking was Bella's life. Becoming a chef had always been her dream. She and Charlotte had managed to finagle Bella her own cooking show, which had failed—as Nestle Bingham was so happy to remind her in his review—miserably.

And now Total. Her restaurant. Her chance to start fresh and create her own path as a chef.

Two huge opportunities to start her restaurant off with a bang by throwing a big swanky party and then hosting the socialite wedding of the season had turned on a dime. Her own stupidity had made these two big chances into another historic blunder. An impossible situation where she had to choose between contacting everyone on her invitation list, including the New York Times food critic, and tell them there had been a mistake then hope they showed up on the correct day—or at all— or disappoint Georgina and her mother, possibly alienating an entire section of big money New York who would never consider using Total for an event in the future.

Not much of a choice. And she had nobody to blame but herself.

How could she have been so foolish? So distracted? So careless?

She knew how. Mason.

His presence in the room when she had been printing the invitations. His presence in her life. Right next door. Always in the way and now magnifying her own tendency to create fiascos.

"It's my fault," she said sternly. So sternly that the other two stopped lamenting and turned towards her. Big fat tears welled up in her eyes as Bella lifted her face from her hands and repeated through trembling lips, "It's all my fault!"

She hopped up and rushed out of the room before Noah or Posie could console her. Past the kitchen and the delicious scent of Posie's flan, past the empty bar with its shimmering rows of clean glasses, past the tables set and ready for the day's customers, and up to the cash register. Her beloved restaurant, blurry though it was through her tears, was still so beautiful. This made the tears flow heavier.

Bella couldn't stop crying. It was a deep cry, that's what her mother would have called it. No wailing or sobbing, just a constant flow of uncontrollable tears and a face twisted in anguish.

The tears came from someplace hollow inside of her soul. A place that she tried to ignore, but that never went away. Quiet and dark, hardened to the beauty in the world, this place in her soul greeted every blessing with a cold hard dose of reality.

"Stupid, stupid, stupid," Bella hissed as she pressed both palms against her forehead.

"Bella, try to calm down." Noah approached her from behind and put his hand on her shoulder.

The interruption of her downward spiral was startling and Bella jumped at his touch. She yelped and her arms flailed into the air, brushing the carefully placed Christmas garland above and sending Mason's Christmas spider tumbling first into her hair and then to the floor.

She stared at the sparkling arachnid. The sight of it awkwardly askew at her feet triggered a deep frustrated rage and she had to fight the urge to crush it under her heel. Bella wanted to scream, to stomp, to hit something, break something, expel everything she was feeling through a violent physical action.

Instead she took in a deep breath, then another, exhaling through pursed lips. Without a word to Noah, or to Posie standing behind him, Bella leaned down and scooped up the Christmas Spider then stuffed it unceremoniously back into the garland hardly caring if it was secure enough to keep from falling again.

Both Noah and Posie watched her carefully, like she was a firecracker about to explode. The tears had finally stopped streaming from her eyes and Bella wiped her cheeks with the back of her hand, sniffing heavily, trying to regain her composure.

"I'm sorry, I'm sure every—" she was interrupted by the sound of the front door opening. She whirled around to see Mason smiling widely at them.

"Good morning!" His happy greeting was quickly followed by concern. "Is everything okay?"

"We've had some bad news..." Posie began to explain, but let her voice trail off when Bella shot her a look.

"Everything's fine," Bella insisted. "Nothing that we can't handle."

Mason switched his gaze to each of their faces, not sure if he should believe her, but not really in a position to argue.

"Just a little decoration malfunction," Noah motioned to the gnarled garland and the crooked Christmas spider.

Mason lifted his eyes to the spider and guilt pricked at Bella. She had almost smashed the thing to smithereens moments ago. That would have been an awkward scene for him to walk in on.

"What are you up to today?" she asked him brightly. A little too brightly, probably.

He gave her a queer look before answering, "Heading to the gym."

She took in his sweats and the black gym bag slung over his shoulder. "Boxing?"

He nodded. "I was gonna see if you wanted to go with me. Try it out."

"Boxing?" Noah chuckled as if he couldn't imagine Bella going to a sweaty gym, lacing up boxing gloves, and punching someone.

Bella stood riveted to the floor staring at Mason like an inventor who had just come up with a possibly brilliant idea. Images of gloved hands smashing into punching bags ran through her head.

"Yes," she said, much to the surprise of everyone. Especially herself.

"Yes?" Mason looked closely into her eyes, his smile slowly returning.

She nodded, more certain as each moment passed that

she needed to get away from her latest mistake and hit something...hard. Even if Mason was the one escorting her. "Yes, I want to try it out." She glanced back at Noah and Posie's shocked faces. "I'll be back soon and we'll figure everything out."

Without another thought, Bella grabbed her coat and walked out of her restaurant.

CHAPTER 14

While they walked to Bella's apartment, Mason didn't say a word about her sour mood.

He waited patiently in the combination living and dining room as she rummaged through her closet and shoved a pair of yoga pants, tennis shoes, and a green T-shirt into her hot pink gym bag. He didn't ask what was bothering her or try to get her to explain her tear stained cheeks and puffy eyes as they made their way several blocks to his boxing gym.

All he did was make pleasant small talk about the weather, little comments like, "It sure is cold even for December" and "They say we may get another big snow before Christmas".

Bella's whole body was tense. Her jaw was set tightly. Occasionally a tremor moved through it from all of the anxiety built up in her system. Stepping firmly, almost stiffly, she kept her eyes ahead, focusing hard on not bumping into anyone or anything.

Meanwhile, Mason kept their one sided conversation going with his little weather platitudes. She was grateful for that much. She knew if she did try to speak the tears might come again, and this time she didn't know if she could stop them. She needed a distraction, a release. It appeared that Mason sensed this, too, and was happy to oblige with this boxing excursion. Hopefully the activity would be enough to snap her out of her gloom.

The gym was in an old white stone building with thick glass windows that were fogged up on the inside from all of the body heat. The indoor humidity was so high that water built up along the top edges of the window panes until it dripped down making rivulets in the foggy glass

"After you," Mason said pulling open thick wooden double doors.

Bella walked in and heavy air warmed her cheeks immediately. It smelled like chlorine, leather shoes, and men. Two well built men stood behind an old wooden counter with a string of fat Christmas lights haphazardly hung across the front. They smiled at her with peaked interest then spied Mason following.

"Povich, you bring your own nurse this time?" the shorter man asked with a smirk.

"She's here to work out, moron," Mason teased back.

"Oh, well that's another story," the short man said, smiling as he pushed a clipboard with a visitor's sign in sheet towards Bella.

Mason pulled a brown paper grocery sack out of his gym bag and plopped it onto the counter, much to the delight of the two men. The sweet smell of barbecue sauce emanated from the bag.

"There's enough in there for six people...so you two should be good until break time," Mason joked. The men laughed and agreed as they pulled sandwiches out of the bag.

Marble steps flanked by carved wooden banisters led to a second story and the women's and men's locker rooms. Mason dropped her off at the door of the women's locker room with a bashful duck of his head. When she emerged dressed in her workout clothes he was waiting. Leaning against the wall, strong arms and well defined stomach muscles apparent in his snug t-shirt. He looked fit and healthy. The kind of fit and healthy that made the gym's warm temperature seem even warmer.

When he saw Bella his eyes wandered down her body before he caught himself and shifted his attention back to her face. Checking her out in her yoga pants no doubt. Bella was a little flattered and smiled in spite of her doom and gloom attitude.

"I guess I'm ready," she said.

"You're ready. I have a feeling you're really gonna like boxing." He grinned, pushing off the wall and falling in step beside her as they went up the stairs to the third floor, his gym bag still slung over his shoulder.

Bella was not prepared for what met them at the top.

The whole floor was one giant room lined with the same foggy antique windows that were on the first floor. The space held two honest to goodness boxing rings, one on each end. Lifted off the floor, bordered by the same thick ropes she had seen in movies tons of times, but realized she had never seen in person. Lines of tear shaped leather speed bags ran along the wall and evenly spaced black punching bags hung in every open space in between.

For some reason she hadn't thought they were going to an authentic boxing gym. She was thinking more of an everyday gym that had some boxing bags set up near the free weights. The kind that had neon footprints taped to the floor to show you where to stand.

There was definitely no neon in Mason's boxing gym.

What was there, in addition to all of the intimidating–if worn out–equipment, were men. Lots and lots of men.

Men of every size, shape, and color pounded the punching

bags, slammed the speed bags so rapidly they blurred, and shuffled back and forth, gloves raised in front of their faces, as they faced each other in the ring. The one thing they all had in common was impressive muscles, which flexed and rippled as they moved.

The noise was deafening.

The show of strength and potential brutality was formidable.

Bella's steps slowed as they reached the top of the stairs. Mason noticed and slowed with her.

"Are women allowed in here?" was her first question.

"Of course."

Bella scanned the room. "I mean, is there a women's section or something..." her voice trailed off as she spotted two women working on one of the bags.

They weren't as tall as most of the men in the room, but what they lacked in height they made up for in intensity. One of them held her shoulder against the punching bag, facing the other woman and barking words of encouragement, or maybe they were insults, Bella couldn't tell. The other woman kept her focus on the bag, glaring at it and pummeling it so fast and so hard Bella winced a little as each hit landed.

If that was the women's section Bella wasn't sure she measured up.

Mason followed her gaze and tried to reassure her, "There's no women's section. It's co-ed."

"Oh," Bella swallowed.

"Come on, Mo always has some extra gloves.

Mo turned out to be the manager of the gym. An older Black man whose only indication of his age was the tiniest sprinkling of grey at his temples. The rest of him was just as fit and toned as every other man in the room, including his left bicep which sported a tattoo that read 'Mo Betta'.

Mo happily loaned Bella a pair of black boxing gloves out

of a closet of used equipment saying, "You can hang on to those until you get your own."

Bella wasn't sure she would be getting her own boxing gloves, but appreciated the offer.

"Let's get your hands wrapped," Mason said, pulling what looked like two rolls of thin black yoga straps out of his bag. "Want to sit on the ring and I'll help you?" He pointed at the currently empty boxing ring nearby with his chin. When Bella couldn't quite hop onto it, he took her by the waist with both hands and lifted her up. A move that was both commanding and gentle.

Starting by wrapping the end of the long strap around the palm of her hand, looping in over her thumb and repeating a few times so it wouldn't come loose, Mason continued wrapping up and down her hand and wrist until the long strap came to an end and he secured it by tucking it under the edge. Bella watched. Intrigued by the process and struck by his light touch, she took the few moments he was concentrating on the task to allow her gaze to wander over him.

His hair was charmingly tousled as always. From this angle, with his head bent in front of her, Bella had an unusual view of Mason's ears and neck and she had the ridiculous thought that he had the most attractive ears and neck she had ever seen. Even his plain navy blue t-shirt, worn and faded, couldn't hide his impressive physique. She glanced around the room and realized with a flutter in her chest that he was definitely one of the best looking men in the room.

Again she noticed the two boxing women. They were taking a break from punching the bag to get a drink from their water bottles. One of them saw her looking at them and Bella immediately averted her eyes. She pretended she was looking at the wall just beyond the women where a large digital clock and a sign that read 'The more you sweat the less you bleed' hung. Someone had placed a goofy plastic Rudolph on top of the digital clock.

"All set," Mason said.

Bella looked down at her hands and wrists wrapped in black and the flutter in her belly turned into a small surge of excitement. "Now what?"

Mason held the end of one of his wraps in his teeth while he expertly looped the opposite end around his thumb. "Jup roop," he said.

Bella furrowed her brow, not understanding.

"Jup roop," he said through his teeth again, bending his head towards the far corner of the room where dozens of jump ropes of varying lengths hung from hooks.

"Oh," Bella laughed. "Jump rope!"

And jump rope they did. Bella hadn't jumped rope since she was a child and she didn't remember it being so difficult. Somewhere along the journey from childhood to adulthood she must have lost some coordination.

Mason had not lost anything.

As she struggled to keep from tangling up and falling flat on her face Mason's jump rope whipped through the air so fast it made a high pitched whirring sound. His feet seemed to barely leave the ground yet the jump rope never stopped as it cleared the slim space between the soles of his shoes and the gym floor. The control he had over his body and the jump rope was apparent and Bella would have been more impressed if she wasn't so out of breath.

"Warmed up?" he asked as he stopped jumping and let his rope slow to a stop on the floor in front of him.

Bella nodded her head and gratefully put her jump rope back on its peg. Her heart was pounding and she was panting, but she managed to ask, "When do I get to hit something?"

Mason chuckled, "Soon, I promise."

She followed his lead as he did arm circles, back and leg

stretches, then dropped to the ground for crunches and planks. By the time they were done with the 'warm up' Bella thought they had almost completed a full workout.

"The speed bag," Mason announced after leading her over to the row of tear shaped bags hanging from small platforms. "Have you ever used one of these?"

Bella shook her head 'no'.

"First, they need to be about eye level," he said.

She bent her head back and looked up at the bag in front of her, which was maybe chin level with Mason, but definitely not eye level with her. She made a face.

His eyes danced merrily, enjoying her reaction. "Here, we can fix that."

He reached behind the mount and the speed bag lowered to the appropriate height, which Bella noted was well below any other speed bag in the room. She would have to make up for her lack of height with enthusiasm.

She knocked the bag with her knuckles, mimicking what the men on other bags were doing. The speed bag barely moved and Mason turned his face away from her to hide a laugh.

"Don't laugh at me, just show me how to do it," Bella insisted.

He turned back, the laughter still in his eyes, "You got it."

Mason showed her how to get her rhythm down with the speed bag, though her efforts were childishly slow compared to his. After that he helped her into her borrowed boxing gloves and showed her the right boxing form, elbows bent with gloves in front of her face to block punches. They worked on a punching bag, Mason holding it while she tried the one-two punching he demonstrated. Then Bella held the bag for him and was lifted off the ground every time he landed a blow.

"Sometimes it helps to visualize," he said from behind his

gloves right before his right hand shot out into the bag. "It helps you focus your strength."

"What do you visualize?"

He grinned, "When I first started boxing I pictured the banker who harassed my Mom when she couldn't pay her mortgage." He tapped the black bag with his left glove and stepped back, glaring at the spot. "I just imagined his pale, mean face right there and then–" he stepped forward and punched the bag hard six times in quick succession.

Bella was pushed up and back with each punch. She laughed out loud in surprise.

Mason grabbed the bag with his gloved hands, steadying it and her. "Sorry."

"It's okay," she reassured him. "I can see how this is a major stress relief."

"Yes it is...are you feeling less stressed?" Mason looked at her carefully, still holding the bag, his body very close to hers.

The flutter in her stomach returned for a moment and she looked away from him, letting her eyes wander around the room. Her legs and arms were tired, her whole body was tired, but she definitely wasn't tense anymore.

"I am feeling better," she said.

Mason's eyes twinkled. "Good. I was hoping you would."

Bella squirmed a little under his happy gaze. "I wasn't *that* stressed."

"You weren't?"

She could tell he wasn't buying it.

"No...well, a little." She sighed. May as well let Mason in on her big fiasco. It wasn't like he wouldn't find out about it eventually. She decided to leave out the part about how he had distracted her so much she made the mistake. "I accidentally booked that big wedding we're doing at the same time as our Christmas party."

Mason's eyebrows lifted in shock. He let out a low whistle.

"I know," she grumbled.

"Can you reschedule the party?"

She shook her head 'no'.

"I already mailed all of the invitations." Mason winced, showing he understood while Bella continued talking, letting her worries flow, "It's a nightmare. I don't know if we can pull it off. We don't have the space or the staff. I won't have money to hire and train a lot of staff beforehand. I used everything I had to get the restaurant started up and was going to float on the money from the wedding, but now I think I should cancel so it doesn't turn into a massive debacle and nobody will ever book us for a wedding again..." her voice trailed off and she stared miserably at the floor.

Quiet sat between them as Bella remembered everything she had been so upset about before she walked into the boxing gym with Mason. The exercise had relieved her tension, but explaining it to him was bringing on a different sensation. A low grade sense of doom.

"Is there anything I can do to help?" Mason asked.

She looked up and saw sincere concern in his eyes. But she couldn't think of anything he could do that would improve the situation. She wasn't even worried about his silly Pits sign anymore. She had bigger problems.

"That's nice of you, Mason, but I don't think there's anything you can do. I'm afraid I'm just going to have to take the hit."

Bella raised her gloved hands and barked out a laugh at her pun. Mason smiled politely, but she could tell he didn't find much humor in it.

If she was being honest, neither did she.

CHAPTER 15

Bella was sore all over. On every possible layer of her muscles, her bones, and her soul.

The workout with Mason had been good for her, it had brought her a peace of some kind. However, the next morning as she sat in her office and stared at the realities of the schedule, she knew it was never going to work.

She had slept hard after boxing then returning to work for the dinner shift. When her head hit the pillow that night she went out like a light, which was surprising. She had expected to be flopping and flailing and wrenching her heart in all directions all night long. Pure physical fatigue had done its job.

The next day she arrived early in the hopes that looking at the problem in the morning light might bring fresh ideas to her mind. Maybe one of Santa's elves had snuck in over night and fixed her problems, or the Christmas spider had pulled off some kind of magical change.

But there was no way.

After poring over her available resources and the timing of the events, Bella knew she had to make a hard decision.

She could not afford to fail at both the Christmas party and the wedding, so she had to choose one.

Mason had offered his help, as had Noah and Posie. Even with them and Manuel and all of her new staff who were dedicated to the idea of making Total unique and putting it on the map, there was no getting around the truth. She didn't have the money, the space, or the staff to throw a party and a wedding at the same time.

She decided that since her invitations were already sent out for the party, the wedding was on the chopping block. But before she did that, she needed to make sure the wedding hadn't had its own invitations printed and sent yet. If the wedding guests had already been notified, she would have to swallow her pride and tell Nestle Bingham that she was canceling her party, and probably lose out on any possibility of his good graces forever.

With a heavy heart, she lifted her cell phone and punched Georgina's name. The call rang through to voicemail and as Bella listened to the message she took in a deep breath and steadied herself. At the beep, she spoke.

"Hi, Georgina this is Bella from Total. I have an urgent update about the plans for your wedding and I need to speak to you right away. It's very important that you call me back as soon as possible. Thank you, goodbye."

Bella turned the cell phone face down on the desk with a thud and dropped her head, letting out an exasperated sigh. "Ugh. I can't believe this is happening."

Depressed, she took her phone and left the tiny office to busy herself with something mundane while she waited to hear back. She wished Georgina had answered so she didn't have to endure the stomach churning anxiety of someone about to deliver bad news.

After straightening the receipts next to the cash register she let loose an exasperated sigh and turned around in a circle looking for something else distracting to do. Her eyes landed on the Christmas spider sitting askew in the garland above the register.

"A lot of good you've done me," she said to the spider. She narrowed her eyes and stared at it unpleasantly. The Christmas spider remained still, sparkling in defiance.

She thought about Mason and his twinkling eyes. The way he had palpably felt bad for her when she explained her sour mood to him. He had been sweet to offer his assistance, though she knew there was little he could do. She could hardly send either her Christmas Eve party or Georgina's wedding to eat barbecue at Pits on Christmas Day.

Yet his support had meant something. It wasn't just the boxing that had calmed her down. Being near Mason calmed her. He made her feel like there was more to her life than merely constant difficulties stacking up, one on top of each other.

She looked at the Christmas spider again and if she didn't know better she would swear his little eight-legged body was tilted sympathetically, as if he was concerned about her plight.

"Oh brother," she reached up and straightened him so he was no longer shoved in the garland like a discarded ornament, but sitting prettily on it. "I guess it can't hurt to give you another chance."

Her cell phone rang. Bella winced. Her palms were sweaty as she took the phone from her pocket. She was not looking forward to this conversation. But when she saw the name buzzing through, all of her reservations fell away. Charlotte.

"Charlie!" Bella answered with relief.

"Bella, guess what?" Charlotte's voice was a welcome sound.

"I'm in no mood for guessing games. You don't know what's been going on here for the last few days."

"What's going on?"

Bella let out a groan, "I've made a mess of things. Again."

"What did you do?" Charlotte asked with concern.

Bella explained the booking problem and how she didn't have the time or money to take care of it. She told Charlotte she was going to have to disappoint Georgina.

Charlotte's voice dropped with concern. "Oh no...well, now I don't know how my news is going to grab you."

"What's your news?"

"Um...we are here," Charlotte said.

Bella didn't quite understand. "Here...here? *Here?* Here in New York? Here in the city?"

Charlotte giggled. "Yes, here in the city. And here at your restaurant."

"What?" Bella looked around as if Charlotte and Davis were hiding behind the bar about to jump out and yell surprise.

"Out front. Across the street." Charlotte laughed at Bella's surprise.

Bella rushed to the front door, opening it wide and letting in a cold burst of air. There were a number of pedestrians and traffic in the street, but it only took Bella a moment to find her best friend happily waving at her.

Short and round with long black hair tucked under a white hat, Charlotte was hard to miss in the bright winter sunshine. Her royal blue coat with white trim stood out amidst the grey and black clad New Yorkers.

Bella squealed with excitement at the sight of Charlotte and Davis. In a few short minutes they were nestled in at Total's front table sipping hot cocoa and explaining their presence in the city.

"The family that was supposed to stay at the Inn for two weeks had to cancel," Charlotte began.

Davis, boyishly handsome and as unassuming as ever,

nodded along with his chirpy wife's story as he sipped his hot cocoa.

"What happened?" Bella asked.

"There was some kind of car accident involving the Grandma and one of the grandchildren," Charlotte said, her pretty face frowning at the tragedy of it all. "They're okay… sort of. They're going to be okay, I should say. But they're both still recovering, not really up for travel. And the family didn't want to leave them behind…so they canceled."

"That's too bad," Bella said.

"Too bad for them," Davis added. "But not really for us."

"True," Charlotte agreed. "We've been booked solid since last Christmas. Which is great on one hand, of course."

"Good for the bank account," Davis agreed.

"But not so good for us. We just really needed to get away and go somewhere different. Somewhere exciting." She smiled widely at Bella. "New York seemed like a perfect trip!" Charlotte let her eyes wander around Total. "Oh, Bella, this place is beautiful!"

Bella smiled at the compliment then a question struck her, "Did you bring the dogs?"

Davis and Charlotte shared a smile. They loved their two dogs, Bailey and Bacardi, almost like they were children.

"Bill's watching them for us. And the horses. His daughter's coming up for the holiday with him and they'll have the whole place to themselves," Davis answered.

"So we're here without the fur babies and ready to help you with your party," Charlotte declared. "Or the wedding, maybe? Whatever you need us to do."

Relief washed over Bella and she sank back into her chair. "It would be great to have your help, but I don't want you to work on your vacation."

"It's not work if you love it," Charlotte reminded her.

"I'm happy to help, too," Davis added with a warm smile.

Bella was grateful for her friends. They did have particular skills given that they ran a successful Inn in the Rocky Mountains, plus there was Charlotte's extensive design background. But she wasn't sure how much they could actually change the outcome of her particular plight.

As she considered their offer, Bella was distracted at the sight of Mason waving at her through the window and making his way to her front door. She looked quickly back to her friends, but not quick enough for Charlotte not to notice her reaction to seeing him.

Mason opened the front door and stepped in. "Good morning, am I interrupting?"

Bella started to answer, but Charlotte chimed in first, "No, no, not interrupting at all." She gave Bella a knowing look.

Introductions were made in a flurry as Bella tried to act nonchalant, but Charlotte kept giving her the secret friend smile. That smile women share when they know one of them has a crush.

"I don't want to crash your get together," Mason said. "But I had an idea and I wanted to run it by you."

"Okay," Bella said, only slightly hesitant.

"You know our Christmas day dinner that we're doing?" he asked.

Bella suddenly remembered the big dinner giveaway and the lines of needy people that they expected to serve at Pits on Christmas day. She hadn't even thought about that part of the fiasco. Her stomach sank like a rock.

She cleared her throat and tried to act like this wasn't another problem in her ever growing list of problems. "Yes?"

Mason's face lit up as he continued, "I happen to know a number of our regulars personally."

"Okay..." Bella didn't know how to respond to this information.

"And there are a lot of them that have worked in the restaurant industry." Mason watched for her reaction and, not seeing enough of one, he continued, "Really talented servers and cooks. Really good people who are just out of work right now."

Bella tried to wrap her mind around what he was saying. Mason looked from her to Charlotte to Davis and back to Bella. Still she didn't know what to say.

"I was thinking if you needed extra hands on Christmas day, I could get all the extra people you need without you having to hire on any permanent employees." He looked at all three of them with merry eyes.

"Oh," Bella finally grasped the new information.

"Bella," Charlotte said, her voice bubbling with excitement. "If I'm here to help with the wedding, and Davis can be kind of your assistant manager to help with the party, and," Charlotte lifted her hand towards Mason, "Mason here has extra staff that you can use...maybe you don't have to cancel anything."

A tiny thrill of hope rippled through the room as the four of them embraced the possibility. Bella's heart beat rapidly in her chest. Just a few minutes ago she had been ready to give in, but suddenly everything felt different. Maybe the situation wasn't so bleak after all.

Bella's cell phone rang, bringing her back to reality. She looked at it and saw Georgina's name.

"It's Georgina...the bride," she announced. She froze.

"Don't cancel," Charlotte insisted. "I'll help you. We'll all help. We can figure it out."

Feeling a little bit like a gambler who was about to bet it all, Bella made her decision.

"Okay, we'll do it," she said. A rush of excitement swelled in the room. Bella looked at her ringing phone. "But what do I tell her?" She looked to the others for suggestions. "I told her to call me back because of something urgent."

"Tell her you've flown in an additional designer for the wedding," Charlotte said, her voice dancing. "Then give me the phone."

CHAPTER 16

The next few days blew up into a fun flurry of activities and planning. Charlotte, Davis, Mason and Eddie joined forces with Bella, Noah, Posie, and the rest of Total's staff to throw three huge events on the same day. All of them energized with the Christmas spirit.

With her short red hair poking out from under a blue and white snowman scarf she had wrapped around her head while baking, Posie joyously compared their impossible goal to space travel, "It's like we've decided to fly to the moon...and we actually might make it!"

"Why not? Santa makes reindeer fly this time of year, why can't we do the impossible?" Charlotte added.

"Right, why not?" Bella agreed.

Their first order of business was to determine where each event would occupy each space.

"What time is your Christmas dinner wrapping up at Pits?" Davis asked Mason and Eddie.

Davis had taken on a kind of a go-between general manager role to handle all of the higher level logistics. He conducted a planning meeting as they all sat at Total's bar late at night after closing.

"Our Thanksgiving meal was over by five. That's what we were planning on for Christmas, too," Eddie answered.

"We'll stop cooking by three thirty," Mason added. "We feed everyone what's left and then close the doors."

Davis nodded, pleased with this information. "Good, that means we could use your kitchen starting at three thirty?"

Mason looked at Eddie for verification before answering, "Absolutely."

"That's great! Two operational kitchens will make a huge difference," Noah said, his state of high anxiety visibly diminishing as that part of the logistical puzzle became clear.

"That still doesn't solve our space problem," Bella said. "We only have the main floor dining area and the second floor banquet room. We were planning on having the wedding on the second floor then come down here to have the reception."

"But now this space will be needed to host the Christmas party," Charlotte clarified the issue as she looked around Total's main dining room, sizing it up.

"What about the third floor?" Eddie suggested.

All eyes turned to him as he looked at Mason.

"What's on the third floor?" Davis asked.

Mason's face lit up and he slapped Eddie on the shoulder. "That's a great idea!"

"What's on the third floor?" Posie asked, intrigued by the Barbecue Boy's excitement.

"It's in pretty rough shape," Eddie warned.

Mason waved this comment away, obviously delighted with whatever the third floor held, "Naw, we can fix it up in time."

"What's in rough shape?" Davis asked again.

"What needs fixed up?" Bella asked skeptically.

"You have the banquet room on the second floor in your lease, but we have the banquet room on the third floor in our lease," Eddie finally explained. "It kind of got thrown in and we haven't used it yet because it needs fixed up."

"It's not quite as big as the second floor room," Mason warned.

"And it needs fixed up," Eddie reiterated.

Mason looked at Bella, happy to give her good news. "It's got great windows and a better view than the second floor."

"Can we see it?" Charlotte asked right before Bella had a chance to pose the same question.

A few minutes later they all were climbing a narrow set of stairs that led from the back of Pits up to the third floor of their old building. They were back stairs, not meant to be showy. And showy they were not. Bella wasn't sure how they could utilize a space that required any guest to climb up two flights of dark cramped stairs.

At the top they came to a locked door. Mason pulled a ring of keys out of his jean's pocket, opened the door, and ushered them all in as he held the door for them. As Bella passed through the doorway she could tell by the look on his face that Mason was pretty excited about the room.

They stood in the dark for a few moments as Eddie searched for the light switch. Then, suddenly, the whole room illuminated and Bella gasped.

It was a grand old room. Spacious with dark wood floors, the same high ceilings as the first floor, a half dozen chandeliers, and tall arched windows along the outside wall. Truly a beautiful room, but in a state of disrepair.

The paint on the walls was chipped practically everywhere, the wood floors were worn and dirty, two of the chandeliers weren't working, and the windows, though gorgeous, were old and caked with dust and grime.

"This could be gorgeous," Charlotte said.

Bella coughed as the dust in the room got to her. "Do you really think so?"

"It's beautiful," Posie agreed. Though Posie was known for her love of the strange and forgotten, perhaps her opinion might be an overstatement.

Davis walked along one wall to the windows, inspecting the issues. Bella's initial hope for using the room dwindled as she watched him squat down and run his finger along the floorboards. Davis had restored his beloved Crystal Lake Inn himself and she trusted his judgment on whether or not they could bring this room up to snuff. From the look on his face, it didn't look good.

"It needs a coat of paint...or two," Eddie said.

"And the floors need to be redone," Davis added.

"Oh, but it could be so pretty," Charlotte said. "I could fill it up with flowers and lights and candles and drapes and nobody would know it had ever been this neglected."

"Do you like it?" Mason was watching Bella carefully.

She didn't want to sound picky so she chose her words carefully, "It's lovely. I mean, it could be lovely. But I don't know..."

"Any work we do on it would have to be completed in a week," Noah pointed out.

"I can't afford a renovation," Bella said.

"Actually, we've already put aside the money to paint the place, but we haven't had the time to do it," Mason said.

"I could do the floors for the cost of supplies," Davis stood up as he made this announcement.

Bella was shocked, "Really? In a week?"

Davis smiled, "In three days."

They all smiled and watched Bella for her reaction. Since it was her restaurant and two of the events on the line were vitally important to its success, she was the final say on every decision. There was a lot of pressure in that position, but she found the pressure invigorating.

One last issue held her back. The stairs.

"If we can fix it up I say great. But I can't see leading anyone from the wedding or the Christmas party up those awful stairs."

Everyone's excitement faltered except for Mason's.

"No problem," he said, taking her by the hand and leading her to a door at the opposite side of the room. "Your second floor banquet room is connected to this room through another staircase." He used his key to unlock the new door and opened it with the flourish of a magician.

A beautiful wood staircase with carved banisters and antique sconce lighting led down from where they stood into the back door of her banquet room. She could not suppress her smile.

Mason stood near her side, his arm still outstretched as he held the door open. His pleasure at solving her problem was obvious.

She glanced back at the others then up into his eyes, feeling a little giddy at their close proximity.

"Do you know any painters or construction workers who are looking for a temporary gig?" she asked.

Mason grinned. "You bet I do."

Bella was satisfied. She turned back towards her friends and announced happily, "I think this will work."

Posie called out, "Santa, we have lift off!"

Everybody cheered.

***

. . .

MANAGING A RENOVATION, planning a wedding, throwing an opening party, and supporting Pits in their Christmas day meal giveaway created an avalanche of work. The constant coming and going, the meetings, the decisions, the worrying over the budget, all while trying to operate Total on a normal day-to-day basis provided so much to do that time positively flew by. Bella's every moment of every day was packed full, from the instant she woke in the wee hours of the morning until she crawled into bed late at night.

Add in the natural buzz and excitement of the holidays and the air was practically electric. Luckily Bella's employees and friends, both of the old and new variety, stepped up to help.

Charlotte took over all things Georgina and wedding related. The socialite fell in love with Charlotte immediately and was especially captivated by her celebrity status. Chef Charlotte's cooking show had, apparently, been one of Georgina's favorites.

Posie continued working on the extravagant wedding cake design along with all of her normal duties at Total. Noah vetted all of the new temporary employees and managed the details for the Christmas party. Davis headed up the renovation team with Mason and Eddie assisting as needed. This left Bella right where she wanted to be, in the kitchen developing two knock-out menus.

"Davis has a lot of nice things to say about Mason and Eddie," Charlotte said.

She was sitting at the bar working on two different layouts for the reception for Georgina to pick from. The rather busy dinner rush was over and Bella had joined her with her own paperwork, a list of ingredients she needed to order before she went home tonight.

"Hmm?" Bella asked, distracted with her list.

"Mason and Eddie seem really nice...Davis likes them."

Bella looked up to see Charlotte watching her, a meaningful look in her eyes.

"What is that look for?" Bella laughed, pretending she didn't know.

"Oh, come on, Bella, let's have some girl talk," Charlotte pretended to be frustrated.

"Girl talk?"

"You know exactly what I mean," Charlotte teased. She looked around the empty bar and the near empty restaurant. "We haven't had five minutes alone together since I got here for you to tell me what is going on between you and Mason?"

Bella dropped her eyes and studied her list with fresh urgency. "There's nothing to talk about."

"Pshaw!" Charlotte disagreed with a loud snort. "Nothing to talk about." She leaned closer to Bella's bent head and whispered, "This is me, Bella. I know you like him and I can see he likes you, too."

"You can?" This piqued Bella's interest and she tore her eyes away from her list.

Charlotte giggled, "Of course he does. He practically moons over you whenever you're around."

"He does?"

Charlotte narrowed her eyes, skeptical of Bella's reaction. "You honestly haven't noticed?"

Bella's stoic stance folded a little under the pressure of Charlotte's stare. "I've noticed a little bit."

"Ah-ha!" Charlotte giggled and nudged her friend.

"But I don't have time for this kind of nonsense, Charlie." Bella waved her hands around in the air indicating everything from the paperwork in front of her to the dining room to the building and New York City outside. "I'm busy here. I'm building something big."

"Right, right, of course you are," Charlotte agreed. Throwing her arm around Bella's shoulders and pulling her into a sideways hug. "Just try to not be so busy that you don't let something wonderful pass you by. That's all."

"I won't," Bella said.

Charlotte was unconvinced, but she went back to her diagrams, smiling to herself with one final comment, "I'm just saying, Davis likes him."

"Davis likes who?" Davis asked, strolling up to the bar. He had come down the staircase from the third floor and entered the dining room from the back.

"Nobody," Bella said.

"Mason," Charlotte said at the same time.

Davis leaned on the bar and helped himself to the plate of tapas the women were sharing. He nodded as he chewed, grunting with satisfaction, then swallowed and agreed with his wife, "Mason's a good guy."

Charlotte smiled meaningfully at Bella, who wanted to crawl under the bar stool. Instead, she shook her head curtly at her friend and stared so hard at her list of supplies her vision blurred a little bit.

Davis kissed Charlotte on the cheek as he swept up two more tapas.

Charlotte wrinkled her nose in jest, "You're dusty."

"I'm dirty, but I'm done," he answered.

The women were surprised.

"The floors are done?" Bella asked.

"And the painting," he responded.

Filled with relief, Bella had to blink back tears. It was only December 18th. There were days to spare before the final decorating had to be done. With all of the extra help it looked like their plans were going to actually work out.

She could hardly believe it was true.

Her body sank against the bar, the sense of relaxation was overwhelming and she realized she must have been keeping her whole body in a giant tight knot over the past few days.

The uncertainty of how everything would turn out had almost been too much.

She had no words for her friends that seemed appropriate. They had done so much for her, dove in with everything they had to help her accomplish her dreams. She didn't know how she would ever thank them.

Davis, scuffed and dusty, hair messy, wood stain darkening parts of his hands, happily munched on more tapas. Charlotte, extra pencils sticking out of the loose bun on the top of her head, sipped her wine, watching Bella over the rim of her glass.

"Are you all right?" Charlotte asked.

Bella nodded, though she wasn't all right, not completely. Her party and wedding were going to work out, but she couldn't help but think about the horrible vacation Charlotte and Davis must be having.

"You two should not be working this hard," she announced.

Charlotte and Davis glanced at each other and back to her.

"It hasn't been that hard," Davis said.

Bella clucked her tongue. "Look at you!" She flapped her hands up and down in his direction. "You're a mess." Then, pointing at the piles of papers in front of Charlotte, said, "And you—you've been so wrapped up with Georgina and all of this—neither of you have relaxed or seen any sights or had any New York City experiences."

"We'll have time for that," Charlotte reassured her.

"When?"

Davis shrugged, "It's not a big deal, Bella. We don't mind helping."

Bella scowled her disapproval.

"Besides, I still have a ton to do, even if Davis is done," Charlotte said. She lifted the diagrams in front of her as proof. "I have to finish these, double-check on the flowers, order in the extra lighting and candles, and go over the details with the band that will be playing," Charlotte's voice drifted into work mode and she tapped her finger on the bar as if she had forgotten something. "Oh, yes! I also have to find some Christmas decorations for the tables. Something gorgeous that Georgina will be thrilled with...and preferably one of a kind."

"There," Davis said. "What about shopping? Isn't that a New York thing?"

Charlotte gasped with delight, "Yes! Of course, we could go do some shopping and get out to see the sights at the same time."

"Bryant Park." The suggestion popped out of Bella's mouth without any forethought.

"What's that?" Charlotte asked.

Cheeks pinking, Bella mumbled her answer, "They have a Winter Wonderland or Village or something like that with little shops...and an ice skating rink...I guess, I've never actually been. Someone told me about it." She hoped Charlotte would be more interested in the shopping than who told her about it.

"Oooh, that sounds perfect," Charlotte clapped her hands together.

"Great, do you want to go tomorrow mid-afternoon? After the lunch crowd?" Bella asked.

"Sure," Davis answered for both of them.

"You should ask Mason to come with us," Charlotte suggested to her husband, ignoring Bella's pointed stare after she made the suggestion.

"Yeah?" Davis mulled over the idea for a moment. "I can, but I doubt he can make it."

Bella experienced the strange sensation of both elation and disappointment zipping through her stomach. She answered Charlotte's mischievous smile with a stern setting of her jaw. "Right, he does have his own restaurant to run after all."

Davis shook his head in disagreement, "It's not that. He takes off in the afternoon every day I've noticed, but not for Pits. Some kind of standing appointment or date maybe? I didn't ask."

Bella laughed stiffly at Davis' comment before trying to shrug it off, "We certainly don't need him to have fun."

She averted her eyes so she wouldn't catch the secret look of dismay Charlotte gave her. Bella was determined not to care if Mason came with them or not, even though the disappointment in her stomach balled up and sank her mood for the night.

CHAPTER 17

Like a little Christmas village of glass houses nestled in the heart of New York City, Bryant Park's outdoor holiday market was an absolute delight.

Rows of cottage sized shops packed the park space, glowing from within, bursting with anything and everything Christmas. Glittering ornaments, handmade cards, fuzzy knit hats, scarves and gloves, toys, dolls, teddy bears, music boxes, garlands and wreaths made from real pine, as well as hot drinks and candy made just for the season were just some of the offerings. Surrounded by tree lined walkways, the shops were set up adjacent to a large open air ice skating rink that perfectly topped off the Christmas feeling.

The gorgeous little specialty shops beckoned to them the moment they arrived, especially Charlotte. Bella accompanied her into every single one of the shops along the first walkway. Merchants offered samples of fudge and hot apple cider as Charlotte 'ooh-ed and ahh-ed' over their wares.

"How many of these do you have?" Charlotte asked a salesgirl at the garland shop, lifting a small wreath made completely of cranberries up for her to see.

"We have about four dozen more of those," the girl answered.

"I'll take all of them," Charlotte said.

The girl's eyes popped at the request, but she happily managed the transaction. So it went in every little glass shop Charlotte visited. She managed to find something she wanted for the wedding in each one and usually cleaned out their stock of the item. This made her a fast favorite as they moved along the first row of vendors. It also made for some heavy lifting.

"Um, I love you honey, but we'll need a small pickup truck to haul everything back if you keep this up," Davis teased as they turned down the next row of shops. His arms were already full of festive shopping bags stuffed with goodies.

Charlotte laughed apologetically, "I'll see if they can deliver anything else I get to the restaurant."

Davis leaned down and kissed his wife on the cheek and an unexpected twinge of melancholy pinged Bella's heart.

Charlotte and Davis had an enviable marriage, full of fun and tenderness, but seeing them together had never made Bella feel sad. Yet here she was standing in the middle of a lovely Christmas outing with a tiny little unexplained heartache in her chest.

She looked away before they noticed something was wrong, but as she glanced around at the other shoppers it seemed that all Bella could see were couples. Bundled up against the cold and strolling arm-in-arm, gazing into each other's eyes, posing cheek-to-cheek for selfies, laughing couples in love enjoyed the holiday festivities. She could not find anywhere to look where some couple wasn't doing something adorable for her to watch with growing misery.

Spying what looked like a shop selling baked goods and hot drinks, Bella announced, "I'm going to go get a hot chocolate. Can I get you some?"

Charlotte and Davis declined her offer and went back to Charlotte's shopping spree as Bella escaped into a world she understood. A world of food.

Being all glass, the bakers doing the work inside the little bakery were in full view. As Bella stood in line breathing in the delicious scent of mini pecan and mincemeat pies, brightly decorated snowman and snowflake shaped sugar cookies, and candy cane brownies, she watched the two bakers joshing with each other as they enjoyed their work. The scene reminded her of how Mason and Eddie joked with each other constantly and she felt another wave of melancholy.

"Stop it," she mumbled under her breath. She didn't need Mason with her to have a good time and she shouldn't allow being single during the holidays to make her depressed.

She had all kinds of things to be grateful for and to keep her busy. Bella scowled as she pushed the thoughts of Mason out of her mind.

"What can I get you?" the man behind the counter asked.

"A candy cane brownie and hot chocolate," Bella said. She would drown her feelings in chocolate.

The man swiftly slipped a chunky square of candy cane brownie into a slim paper bag and poured her a cup of hot chocolate from a large copper urn that had a Santa face on the front.

"Whipped?" he asked, holding up a large piping bag. She nodded and he expertly piped a fat circle of fresh whipped cream on top of the steaming hot chocolate.

Music from the ice skating rink tinkled through the air as Bella sipped from her paper cup. The fresh whipped cream was amazing, but made it difficult to drink without getting a dot of whipped cream on the tip of her nose.

Bella made her way through the crowd to chairs set up on the edge of the ice skating rink. One of her favorite carols,

Santa Claus is Coming to Town, played and was the perfect backdrop for the lively skaters circling the rink. She tried to avoid watching any couples and instead focused on the families with little children. Dressed up in puffy warm snowsuits, some of the children wobbled precariously as they learned how to balance on ice while others overtook their wobbly parents having surpassed their skills.

Bella took a bite of the candy cane brownie and sighed contentedly. Chocolate really was the answer to her mood. She eyed the giant Christmas tree on the edge of the rink and saw that there was space to stand along the edge and watch the skaters from a better angle. She moved to that spot, thinking she would take a few minutes to finish her snack and let the view build up her Christmas spirit. There was no reason in the world that she should moon over Mason's absence. It's not like they were a couple or anything.

She took another sip. As she enjoyed the sensation of smooth chocolaty goodness warming her belly, Bella's eyes wandered across the ice skating rink, taking it all in. Suddenly, she saw something that made her freeze.

She blinked. Twice.

She squinted through the steam coming off of her cup, not sure if she was seeing things. Had all of her longing for a romantic partner to stroll around with sent her into hallucinations? Had Charlotte's teasing about Mason gone to her head?

She didn't know. What she did know was that someone who looked just like Mason was skating, quite well, with a tall blonde woman on the other side of the rink. They were more than skating, they were doing some kind of ice skating routine. Steering clear of the other skaters, they bobbed and weaved and twirled with each other in a way that could only be practiced.

Bella stood motionless, still holding her hot chocolate in

front of her mouth, staring in surprised dismay as the couple moved closer and closer to her side of the rink.

"Bella!" Charlotte called to her from behind, the sound ringing through the air.

The man she thought might be Mason snapped his attention toward Charlotte's voice and Bella knew without a doubt that it was him. From her vantage point at the Christmas tree, Bella watched as Mason saw Charlotte and Davis then scanned the crowd, presumably, for her.

Panicked, Bella turned away from the ice, afraid he might see her staring at him and his date. Afraid he might think she was following him. She cursed under her breath. Why had she even brought up Bryant Park as a destination? He was going to think she was obsessed with him.

"Hey, you!" Charlotte called out again. She and Davis were only about 10 feet away from her, making their way with all of their bags to join her by the tree.

Bella winced. Charlotte's voice seemed to cut through the outdoor noises and echo across the rink. They reached her, Charlotte babbling on and on about some handmade ribbon she had found while Davis gave Bella a curious look. He opened his mouth as if he was going to say something to Bella, but Charlotte interrupted him, her attention drawn to the rink.

"Mason!" Charlotte called out, waving her white fuzzy mittened hand excitedly. "Yoo-hoo! Mason!" She smacked Davis on the arm happily. "Mason's here, do you see him?"

"Yes, honey," Davis grinned.

Charlotte squeezed Bella's arm, eyes wide with fun. "Mason's here!"

Bella nodded, still unable to think of what to do or say. Mason was, it seemed, definitely here. But he was with another woman. Couldn't Charlotte see that?

Charlotte's brow puckered as she looked at Bella's expression. She leaned in to say something, but didn't have a chance.

"Fancy meeting you here," Mason's voice came from the ice.

Bella whirled around to face him.

He was gliding swiftly toward them, a wide smile on his handsome face. Just as she thought he might run into the side of the rink, he turned his feet, expertly cutting the blades of his skates against the ice and coming to a dramatic stop right in front of her.

"Oh, hi," she said. As if she had just realized he was there. As if it didn't make one difference to her that he was. As if her heart wasn't going a hundred miles a minute.

He cocked his head down at her, amused. "How's your hot chocolate?" he asked.

Bella looked down into her cup and back up. To her surprise he reached up and touched the tip of her nose with his finger.

He grinned and said, "Whipped cream."

Bella blushed furiously and hurried to brush away anything else that might be stuck to her face, like brownie crumbs or pure mortification.

"I shouldn't have gotten the whipped cream," she murmured.

He cocked his head again at her, questioning her logic. "Nothing wrong with enjoying your whipped cream," he said with a little wink.

She fought back a smile.

"What are you guys doing here?" Mason asked, sweeping Davis and Charlotte into the conversation.

Bella tried to gather herself while they chatted. She needed to control herself. She shouldn't flirt with Mason while he was on a date. Where was his date? Bella leaned slightly to the side so she could look around Mason for the blonde woman. She was not behind him or anywhere near him for that matter, but rather doing neat spins in the center of the ice.

At first Bella was relieved that she didn't have to make polite conversation with the woman. Just the thought of him being on a date made her cringe. But after a few minutes of him casually talking and laughing with Davis and Charlotte, and occasionally leaning closer to her to say something charming, something irresistible, something he shouldn't be saying to her while he was on a date with someone else, displeasure seeped into her mood.

Bella's face wrinkled into an indignant scowl and she lifted her voice higher than the conversation, "Where is your date?"

All eyes turned to her. Charlotte and Davis were understandably confused, but Mason's innocent expression only infuriated Bella more.

"My date?" he responded.

"Your date? Remember her? You were skating together," Bella pointed an accusing finger at the space over his shoulder indicating the ice rink.

Still unashamed of his behavior, Mason chuckled as he nodded in understanding and said, "Oh, you mean the blonde."

Bella didn't like how he was dismissing the woman and had an urge to defend her. Furrowing her brow and retorted, "She's very beautiful."

"You think so? She thinks she is, too," he chuckled again.

Shocked at his comment, the only response Bella could come up with was a derisive snort.

"You're on a date?" Charlotte asked. Her disappointment on Bella's behalf was obvious, to Bella at least.

"I'm—" before Mason could finish, the blonde came out of nowhere and whipped a neat circle around him, the sound of her blades crisp on the ice.

"Break's over," the blonde said to Mason. He waved her off, but she insisted, "C'mon, we have a lot of work to do."

Mason frowned at her, "Hey, be polite."

Bella could not believe what she was hearing. Was he scolding her?

The blonde took another turn around Mason then paused, looking at Bella, then Charlotte and Davis, as if she had just noticed they were there.

Up close she was even more beautiful than Bella had thought. Tall and lithe, even under several layers of winter outerwear, anyone could see she had a lovely figure. Her blonde hair was thick and long, flowing in undulating waves down to the middle of her back. Bella was instantly intimidated by her good looks; a wide mouth, high cheekbones, and gorgeous sea green eyes.

"Mavis, I'd like you to meet Bella, from the restaurant next to Pits, and her friends, Charlotte and Davis," Mason said.

All of the introduced parties nodded and 'hello-ed' each other. All except Bella. She was still silently fuming.

"Everyone, this is Mavis...my sister."

Bella's hostility turned to confusion.

"Oooohh...your *sister*," Charlotte cooed. Bella refused to look in Charlotte's direction.

Mavis smiled a winning smile, much like her brother's. "Nice to meet you all." She turned her attention fully onto Bella. "You're Bella?" Mavis gave her brother a meaningful look then offered her hand to Bella for a handshake. "I've heard about...your restaurant."

Bella shook Mavis' hand silently, still trying to wrap her mind around her mistake.

"You're practicing an ice skating routine?" Charlotte asked.

"Yes, my regular partner is away for the holidays. So

Mason is taking his place for a little fun competition coming up," Mavis grinned at her brother.

Mason gave a cocky smile and said, "Yeah, helpin' the kid out. You know how it is."

"Stop, you love it and you know you do," Mavis teased.

"Do you ice skate?" Mason leveled his gaze at Bella.

"She does," Charlotte volunteered. Bella widened her eyes at her friend. Charlotte insisted, "Well, you do."

Bella nodded, "Yes, a little."

"Will you come skate with me?" Mason asked. Everyone looked at her again for a response.

She shook her head 'no', "You're practicing."

Mavis jumped in, "We're pretty much done anyway. I can practice my footwork without this lughead."

"You should skate, Bella," Charlotte urged.

"C'mon, Bella, it'll be fun," Mason said. Bella couldn't look him in the eye, but the sound of him saying her name pulled on her heart,

The unmistakable intro to Mariah Carey's 'Christmas' song pumped out of the speaker.

Mason reached out his hand, "This is a great song."

Suddenly, a new excuse popped into her head, "I don't have any skates!" There. He couldn't argue with that.

Mason grinned, "You won't need skates."

"Can't you rent skates?" Charlotte tried to be helpful.

"What are you talking about? How can I do it without skates?" Bella asked.

Mason moved closer, his hand still outstretched. She couldn't avoid his merry green eyes anymore and once they caught her gaze, she couldn't look away.

His mouth lifted on one side like a naughty Christmas elf and he said two words that she found unable to refuse.

"Humor me."

CHAPTER 18

As soon as Bella took his hand Mason drew her as close to the edge of the rink as she could get without stepping onto the ice. He looked down into her eyes and she could not bring herself to protest.

He bent down and spoke so quietly only she could hear, "Ready?"

Before she could ask what she was supposed to be ready for, he let go of her hand and put both of his hands on her waist.

"Ready?" he asked again, waiting for her permission. Suddenly she understood. He was going to carry her.

The music swelled, catching her up in the moment. Bella nodded her permission. One moment later she was floating through the air, almost flying. Mason raised her so high she was looking down at him, her hands on his shoulders.

He took off skating. Fast. They whizzed through the crowd of other skaters but all Bella saw was a blur. An icy breeze tingled on her cheeks.

She laughed out loud, which only encouraged him. His eyes twinkled and she knew he was about to do something even crazier. His body shifted under hers and she could both feel and hear the blades of his skates turning on the ice. Mason completed three full twirls with Bella still held securely above him.

They spun so fast her long hair flew in bouncing tumbles across her face. Mariah sang about all the fun she had last year and the music blended with the scenery rushing past.

Mason's strength was obvious, there was no wavering in his support of her in the air or in the way he moved swiftly across the ice. This was the closest Bella had ever felt to being in a movie...and she had starred in her own cooking show.

"You're crazy," she exclaimed, laughing.

With one fluid move Mason swung her to the side and brought her back down into his arms, this time carrying her like she was his bride and they were crossing the threshold into their honeymoon suite.

"You have no idea," he said with a grin and took her on another spin around the rink.

Bella wrapped her arms around his neck for support and also because she liked the sensation. Resting in his arms felt natural, as if they had done this a hundred times.

The song ended and a rendition of Winter Wonderland started up.

Mason sang to her, "Sleigh bells ring, are you listening? In the lane, snow is glistening..."

Bella laughed again and he bounced gently to the tune as they skimmed across the ice, Mason occasionally moving in a circle with a flourish for her enjoyment. When it got to the line, "Are you married, we'll say no man, but you can do the job when you're in town," Mason wiggled his eyebrows up and down and winked comically. She smacked him lightly on the chest.

As the song ended Mason said, "So, I could carry you

around all night if you want. Or we could get you some skates?" He indicated the warming house set up on the edge of the rink with a nod in its direction.

She agreed. Not that she wasn't enjoying being held up against his body and whisked around like a princess, but she wouldn't mind skating a little herself.

"How's that feel?" Mason asked as he kneeled in front of her lacing up her rented skates. "Not too tight?"

"No, they feel good," she answered.

Normally she would have insisted on lacing up her own skates. She was perfectly capable. But the spell he had cast over her as he swept her off her feet and whisked her across the ice still lingered in the air.

If truth be told Bella was thoroughly enjoying watching him bent over her skates tying the long white laces securely against her leg. There was something masculine and sensual in his action, kneeling in front of her and taking care of her… it warmed her heart.

Mason looked up through the mop of hair that had fallen into his eyes. Her heart skipped a beat.

"All good?" he asked.

She nodded and for once did not try to look away and busy herself with something else. The air between them sparkled and Bella didn't want it to end.

Mason paused, looking deeper into her eyes. So deeply that she was sure he could see what she was thinking. Heat rose in her cheeks at the thought. He smiled quietly, stood, and took her by the hand. Gently, tenderly, he pulled her to her feet.

Minutes later they were skating again, side-by-side, holding hands, and to the sound of Mariah Carey's "All I Want for Christmas". The sparkle between them remained.

Mason timed each skate to the rhythm of the song, making Bella feel more like they were dancing than skating.

Other skaters parted to make way for them and Bella didn't know if it was because they were moving so swiftly or they looked as magical from the outside as she felt on the inside.

Mason's skill on skates was impressive. He was smooth, strong, and fast, pulling her past her normal comfort zone. Her heart pounded as they weaved between slower groups of skaters and zoomed past the festive scenery surrounding the rink. Mason held her hand firmly and stayed so close that she knew he was prepared to catch her, or carry her, if she couldn't keep up.

"You good?" he turned so that he was in front of her, skating backwards, pulling her towards the less crowded center of the ring.

"I think so," she laughed nervously. What was he planning?

"Want to do a spin?" Her heart jumped into her throat and he must have seen the terror in her eyes because he let out a good natured laugh. "It's okay, I'll do it. You just have to relax a little and trust me."

Everything melted away except Mariah's singing, the crunchy swoosh of their blades cutting through the ice, and Mason's twinkling eyes. Her heart in her throat, Bella nodded her agreement.

Facing her, Mason led her in a circle at the center of the rink. Then again in a smaller circle. Then again. Each time they completed a circle he shortened the distance between them so that in just a few passes they were close enough for him to put his hands on her waist.

She watched his eyes, too scared to look anywhere else and afraid if she looked away she would miss his cue. The music wrapped around them, the glowing Christmas Village and all of its inhabitants that surrounded the rink spun around and around, the skyscrapers of New York towered above them in all directions. Yet at the center of everything was Mason, gripping her waist and looking down into her eyes.

"Ready?" he asked.

She wasn't ready. She wasn't ready at all. A thrilling fear filled her whole body and she couldn't breathe. Her stomach shuddered with anticipation. She couldn't even speak. Yet Mason held her eyes with his and she dipped her head in a nearly imperceptible nod.

One moment later she was flying up, up, up into the sky, the world spinning into a kaleidoscope of color and sound as Mason's arms held her firmly from below. Bella laughed out loud as everything seemed to twirl out from where she and Mason spun, making them the center of the skating rink, the center of Bryant Park, of New York City, of what felt like the universe.

She looked down at him effortlessly holding her in place while turning in tight circles on the ice. He was laughing, too. A joyful laugh that made the moment even bigger if that was possible. All Bella could think was how much she loved being with him. How much she loved his spirit. How good it felt when they touched.

Then the moment was over. The crescendo of the song ended and Mason slowed their spin, lowering her back to earth.

He was out of breath. So was she. Riding the high of the moment, unable to break eye contact, she slipped down his body until her skates were back on the ice, his hands still around her waist. Her hair was disheveled from blowing around and Mason reached up with one hand to move a lock that had stayed front of her eyes.

An electrical shock zipped through her body at his touch. Mason felt it, too. He hesitated, his fingers barely touching her hair. His hand that was on her waist slid to the small of her back and pulled her into him. Bella gasped.

"Bella…" Mason whispered her name and pushed back the lock of hair. His finger traced lightly down her temple and cheek, his eyes wandering to her mouth.

He was going to kiss her.

The thought jolted Bella out of the sweet swirly sparkly moment and her stomach clenched in fear. A question filled Mason's eyes and he paused.

"Right on!" a voice rang out and startled both of them and when they tore their eyes off each other, Bella and Mason were surprised to find a group of skaters who had stopped to watch them and were applauding the romantic end of their showy spin.

Bella blushed furiously and turned to hide her face in Mason's chest only to question if she should. If she froze at the idea of kissing him maybe turning immediately to him for comfort wasn't exactly fair. For his part Mason didn't seem to mind. He wrapped an arm around her shoulder and waved amiably to the clapping crowd.

"Let's get out of here," he said and led her to the side of the rink.

When they finally rejoined Charlotte and Davis, Charlotte was beaming. Bella, on the other hand, was embarrassed and confused.

"That was amazing!" Charlotte clapped her mittened hands together happily. "You two look so good together."

Before Bella could respond, the pocket in her jacket started buzzing, providing her with a good excuse to avoid any talk about her and Mason. She pulled her cell phone out and saw that she had several missed phone calls and texts. The current caller was Posie.

"Is everything all right?" Bella asked Posie, suddenly realizing she had left the restaurant unattended for far too long. Anything could have gone wrong.

"Everything's fine, but Noah's having a melt down," Posie answered.

"Why?" A thousand possible scenarios raced through Bella's mind. All of them bad.

"Nestle Bingham RSVP'd 'yes' to the Christmas party."

"Oh," Bella reeled back her doomsday reaction. "That's not so bad, is it?"

"Well, maybe, but guess who he's bringing as his plus one?"

"Rosamonde Baudelaire!?" Bella still couldn't believe it as she stood in Total's kitchen surrounded by a small worried audience.

"Rosamonde Baudelaire," Posie confirmed gravely.

Bella looked at Noah for his reaction, which appeared to be nausea. He was pale and wide-eyed as if he was in shock.

Mason had flagged down a cab for them at Bryant Park and ridden back with her, Charlotte and Davis after Posie told her the news over the phone.

"Who, exactly, is Rosamonde Baudelaire?" Davis had struggled to pronounce the name as he raised the question from the back seat of the cab where he sat with Bella and Charlotte. Mason was in the front next to the cabbie, looking equally confused about the two women's distress.

Charlotte and Bella knew the name all too well.

Charlotte leaned around Bella, who sat in the cramped center, hyperventilating, to explain to her husband. "She's a very famous chef, and an even more famous TV producer. She's had all the great shows..." Charlotte looked carefully at Bella before adding, "She was our producer."

Bella had groaned and covered her face with her hands, and they finished out their cab ride in miserable silence.

Standing in the kitchen with all eyes on her for direction, Bella was at a loss. Nothing but dread and anxiety filled her heart and nothing but a string of curse words came to mind to say.

"Rosamonde Baudelaire," Bella repeated. A chorus of sympathetic sounds came from everyone else.

Mason finally ventured a question, "She's that famous?"

"Infamous, more like it," Noah interjected.

A thought entered her mind and Bella scowled. "He's doing this to vex me," she said hotly.

"Who?" Mason asked.

"Nestle Bingham! I mean, why did he have to tell us she was coming? He knows it will..." she searched for the right words, then found them. "Freak me out!"

"Maybe you don't need to freak out," Mason offered. "Maybe it would be a good thing for a famous chef and television producer to eat here?" his voice raised in a hopeful question.

Bella's scowl deepened and she shook her head sharply. "You don't understand. As much as Nestle Bingham's review in the Times could ruin this restaurant," Bella swept her arm in a grand gesture encompassing Total's dining room. "A bad word from Rosamunde Baudelaire could ruin my entire career. Again!"

"Oh..." Mason's shoulders slumped as the full weight of the problem came down on everyone in the room.

Davis looked between Bella and Charlotte, "I get that she was your producer, but what does she have over you that could ruin everything?"

Charlotte patted Bella on the back, "She figured everything out about our show. How I wasn't really a chef...you know," Charlotte looked guiltily around the kitchen at all of the chefs and cooks present. "In the end she wasn't very kind about any of it. She was quite mean and threatening, actually." Charlotte looked sadly at Bella. "Especially to Bella. I never could figure out why she was so hard on you."

Davis grunted his disapproval and muttered, "As if she's never made a mistake? Nobody's perfect."

"A chef like Rosamonde Baudelaire expects perfection," Bella said. "And I was not perfect in that whole scenario."

Davis snorted, "I bet that's not even her real name."

Bella managed a smile. Her blood pressure was through the roof and she could tell Noah, Posie, Manuel, and the others were on edge about this new development, but Davis' down-to-earth humor helped ease the tension a little bit.

"I don't know how to say this," Mason interjected gloomily. "But I think I may have...encouraged him to bring her."

All eyes turned to him.

Shoulders still slouched, head lowered, he looked around at all of them, his gaze finally landing on Bella with a guilty wince.

Bella stared at him. She didn't know the details, but the all too familiar frustration with the way Mason's antics caused her grief rushed through her mind.

"What are you talking about?" she asked.

Mason cleared his throat, stalling no doubt. "I–uh–well, while I was talking to him when the lights went out–"

"To Nestle Bingham?" Bella asked, her stomach twisting into a knot.

Mason nodded sheepishly, "Yes, when I was talking to Nestle Bingham that night he mentioned that he knew your old producer, but she hadn't been invited to Total's opening."

"And what did you say?" Bella asked without caring what the exact words were. What she did care about, the thing that was churning around in her gut, was the fact that somehow, some way, Mason had, once again, crushed her chances of success.

"I didn't know what he meant exactly. I didn't know you ever had a cooking show," Mason tried to explain. "But I do remember he said a long crazy name. So it must be the same person."

The thrill of ice skating with him was fresh in her mind, the feel of his hands around her waist lingered on her skin, yet the magic of their moments on the ice were fast fading away, replaced with the dread of what he had done to bring Rosamonde Baudelaire back into her world.

"What did you say to him?" she asked again, more sternly.

"I told him he should bring her by sometime," Mason admitted. He watched Bella carefully for a reaction, adding quickly, "I didn't know it would cause any problems. I thought the more publicity the better...you know?"

Bella did know. She knew that her confidence was in tatters. She knew that she had the biggest day of her career coming up and Rosamonde Baudelaire would be breathing down her neck the whole time, glaring at her with contempt, turning up her short stubby nose at whatever Bella served because of her past transgressions. She knew that she had to get out of this room and away from Mason.

Without another word, Bella tore her eyes off of his apologetic face, shot a look of despair at Charlotte, and rushed out of the kitchen to hide in the back office.

"Are you all right?" Charlotte asked a while later as she pushed the door open and let a stream of light into the dark little room.

Bella hadn't turned the light on when she ran in and shut the door behind her, choosing instead to allow her body and soul to slip into deep grief while sitting in pure darkness.

"I guess so," Bella sniffed. She had stopped crying several minutes before, but had run out of tissues before that and didn't want to leave the tiny cave office to go search for more in the supply closet.

"Can I come in?"

"Sure," Bella agreed, hoping Charlotte wouldn't turn on the light.

She didn't. She closed the door halfway to let in some of the hallway light and settled into the chair next to Bella's. In the dim grey of the room Charlotte's face was pinched with worry.

"Bell..." Charlotte began.

Bella shook her head, dismissing whatever Charlotte was about to say. "It's all right. I'll be fine."

Charlotte didn't believe her, "You will? You don't look fine."

Bella coughed out a laugh then sighed. "I have no choice. I have to move forward."

"I know, I just wish...I wish this could all be more fun for you."

Bella laughed again, this time more warmly. "Oh, Charlie. It's all my own doing anyway. I bring all of these stresses onto myself." She lifted her hands to either side of her head and pressed her palms against each temple. "Rosamonde had every right to be furious with me about our show."

"Furious with us," Charlotte corrected her.

Bella gave her a kind smile. "With me. I'm the one that didn't respect the title of chef."

"I lied about being a chef, too," Charlotte argued.

"That's different. You didn't know any better." Bella poked her own chest with her forefinger. "I knew better."

Charlotte decided not to argue anymore and moved on to encouragement, "Maybe it won't be so bad. Maybe she'll love your food."

"Maybe," Bella said without much hope.

Charlotte waited a beat, then said, "He feels awful, you know."

"Who?"

"You know who."

Bella couldn't look at her friend. Her heart pumped madly in her chest, but her stomach was in a tight ball. The thought of Mason confused her...confused everything.

"I–I can't deal with him right now."

Charlotte made a sad sound in her throat.

"Don't, Charlie. I just...he just makes me crazy."

"But you guys look so good together. And the skating! You looked so happy."

Sadness washed over Bella again. A deep sadness overpowered the stress and anxiety she was having about Total and the daunting task of impressing Nestle Bingham, Rosamonde Beaudalaire, and throwing Georgina the wedding of the season.

The sadness went all the way to her core and she couldn't explain it to Charlotte. Not exactly. Luckily, Charlotte was one of her oldest and dearest friends and Bella didn't have to explain.

"It's not going to work out with you two, is it?" Charlotte asked sadly.

Bella sighed. "It can't. He's too much...or I have too much going on. Something isn't right. I can't–I can't make a mistake like that, Charlie. I couldn't take it. And I can't fall apart and lose everything I'm trying to build. I simply cannot do that... not again."

"Right," Charlotte sighed, resigned to her friend's decision even if it wasn't what she wanted. "Well, do you want me to tell him to go?"

Bella didn't understand.

Charlotte looked out the door then back at Bella. "He's

out at the bar with Davis, but I think he's hanging around waiting to see you."

Bella's grief wrapped tightly around her heart, slowing it down. A calm determination overtook her other emotions. She wiped her hands across her cheeks to get rid of any sign that she had been crying and stood up. "No, I'll tell him. I think he should hear it from me."

CHAPTER 20

Bella never got around to telling Mason that she couldn't...shouldn't...start a romantic relationship with him. Not in those exact words.

She didn't have to.

He knew.

She saw it in his eyes when she walked out to the bar where he and Davis were having a drink. The way he sank away from her, trying not to invade her space and immediately looking away when she locked eyes with him.

"Got it all figured out?" Davis asked Bella hopefully. When she didn't answer immediately he shifted his attention to Charlotte who was right on her heels.

Charlotte tried to sound positive. "I think all we can do is forge ahead. We'll impress Rosamonde with style and great food and hopefully she'll pull her claws back in."

"That's the spirit," Davis said, smiling happily at Bella. "You're a great chef, Bella. She won't know what hit her."

Bella managed a smile back. She already felt a little more herself out in the front room of the restaurant, candles flickering, tables of customers, the sights and sounds and delicious smells of Total lifting her mood.

"I should get back to work myself," Mason announced. He tipped his glass and drank the last of his beer in one big swig, then nodded politely at Davis and Charlotte before finally looking at Bella.

The tight ball of her stomach loosened just a little when she looked into those gorgeous green eyes. He smiled and her resolve started to slip away.

"I'll see you tomorrow?" he asked.

Bella shrugged noncommittally. "I have a lot to do. You do, too, don't you? With your free Christmas dinner and everything."

Mason's smile remained on his face, but faded from his eyes. "Right, yes, we're both very busy."

"I'll walk you out," Bella announced, feeling the urge to make things more officially not official, but wanting a little more privacy to explain.

They made it as far as the front counter before Mason pre-empted her with his own announcement. "I was going to ask you if you'd like to come to the candlelight service at our church on Christmas Eve..." he didn't quite finish his sentence and she couldn't tell if he was making a statement or asking a question.

"Oh," Bella didn't know how to answer.

Mason searched her eyes for a moment before making an excuse for her, "I suppose you're busy, though."

"Yes, I'll be pretty busy," she agreed.

He dropped his gaze to the floor between them and Bella felt like a bitter old Scrooge, desperately hanging on to her restaurant and her plans, not willing to let go of them for someone else. Positively miserly. But didn't one have to be a miser with their time and energy when they wanted to create something big? Wasn't that the price to pay for success?

She didn't want to hurt him, but she had to make him understand. "With Rosamonde coming–"

"I'm so sorry about that. I really am. I had no idea."

Bella didn't want to sound like she blamed him, though a part of her did. "Look, Mason, I don't blame you. It's just I can't ignore it, you know? I have to face the facts. Everything that needs to get done and everything that could go wrong with it all...there's so much. What Rosamonde or Nestle Bingham or Georgina thinks of Total could mean the end of it. Or it could mean the beginning."

Mason nodded, a sadness seeping into his expression that wrung at her heart.

She sucked in her breath, determined to stay strong. "You've been great, so much help, really," she said, hoping not to create bad blood. "I just can't do all of this without intense focus. I can't afford to get distracted." She waved her hand towards the Christmas Spider that sat observing them from the garland above the cash register. Mason followed her gesture and looked up at the shimmering arachnid as Bella continued, "I can't rely on good luck. If I make another mistake..." she wasn't sure how to end her thought.

Mason's eyes came back to hers and held them for a long moment. Not twinkling and merry like usual, their normal sea green had darkened.

"I get it, I understand," he said. He backed away from her towards the front door. "I wouldn't want you to make a mistake." He turned and opened the door, looking back only once to say, "I'll be next door if you need anything."

Bella watched him step out into the shivering dark and shove his hands into his pockets then make his way across her picture window without looking back or waving or doing some other goofy thing to make her laugh. Her heart felt cold and hard like it was about to crack, but she didn't go after him and she knew she would not be asking him for any more help.

Without Mason around to distract her or cause any kind of upheaval, she could focus on creating delicious food, which was her passion and her escape. Bella tried to soothe herself with that thought.

Somehow, however, in that moment all of her big plans for the next few days and for her future felt empty and shallow.

CHAPTER 21

Bella threw herself into work, diving deep into the recipes for Total's fast approaching events and barely leaving the kitchen the following morning.

For the most part everyone left her alone. Not because she was in some kind of dark mood, but mostly because they were caught up in their own work, trying to get ready for Christmas Day. Or, at least, that's what Bella told herself.

Posie was elbow deep in Georgina's wedding cake. Four tiers, sleek with perfectly smooth icing, a gold and black air brushed design and incredibly detailed edible poinsettias cascading down one side, the cake was a masterpiece. A masterpiece that had to be duplicated, because Posie always made a copy of her wedding cakes...just in case.

Charlotte, with Davis' help, was spending all of her time decorating the two upstairs rooms for the wedding and the reception. She was also fielding all of Georgina's frantic last minute calls and appeasing the socialite's bridal nerves.

Noah was in charge of the Christmas party in Total's main dining room. Busy crossing all of the t's and dotting all of the i's he had to make sure there was ample liquor, staff, and supplies.

"Like this?" Manuel asked as he whipped chopped cilantro into the bowl of goat cheese for the new croquette recipe they were serving at Georgina's wedding.

"Yes, perfect," Bella told him with a smile. Manuel was a fast learner and she trusted him. They had determined he would head up the borrowed Pits kitchen on Christmas Day to prepare all of the delectable tapas for the wedding. He had learned every new recipe quickly and executed them perfectly. With him taking over that responsibility, Bella could breathe a little easier. She would only have the Christmas Party menu in Total's kitchen to oversee on the big day.

"We have a problem," Noah announced as he entered the kitchen through the large swinging door.

Bella stifled a groan. What now? Whenever she started to feel even the smallest sense of relief, another issue rose up out of nowhere. Tomorrow was Christmas Eve. They didn't have any wiggle room left for last minute problems.

"Plates," Noah said. "We need plates."

"Plates?" Bella picked up the knife she had been using to chop cilantro and carried it to the sink.

"Charlotte thought she was using our plates, but we don't have enough for both events."

Bella plugged the stainless steel sink, turned on the hot water and pumped dish soap into it from the dispenser. Bubbles began to form as the sink filled.

"Eddie said we could use Pits' dishware, but it's a little too casual."

At the mention of Pits, Bella tensed. She had sworn to herself not to ask for any more favors from Mason or Eddie. Her mind started racing for alternative plans as she plunged her hands into the hot soapy water.

"Charlotte thought maybe some patterned china for the wedding? She said it doesn't have to match, she can mix it up," Noah offered.

Bella's stomach sank. She couldn't afford to purchase enough china for a wedding.

"I don't know..." she said, trying to think of a way to resolve this problem as she used her thumb to rub down the knife in the soapy water.

"Mason said he may know where to get some," Noah added.

At the mention of Mason's name, Bella's heart skipped a beat and her thumb slipped on the knife. She sucked in her breath sharply.

She knew she had cut herself before she felt the pain, but when she lifted her hand out of the water she was just as surprised as Noah and Manuel at how bad the cut was.

"Stay there!" Manuel said as he reached for a clean towel and rushed to her side.

Blood rippled down her thumb and mixed with the soapy water from the sink, creating rivulets that ran down her arm.

"I've got the first aid kit," Noah called out as he snatched it off the wall and brought it over.

"I'm an idiot," she hissed under her breath.

"It can happen to the best of us," Manuel said as he wrapped the towel around her hand to stem the flow.

Bella scowled as she allowed the two men to treat her wound with disinfectant and wrap it in bandages. The muscles in her arms and shoulders cramped with tension as the realization of what she'd done sunk in. Such a careless mistake was inexcusable. Getting distracted when handling a sharp kitchen knife was cooking school 101.

"Well, you won't be cooking until this heals up," Noah said with authority. She knew he was right, but the thought was simply too much. Her heart sank into her stomach. How were they going to get through all of this if she couldn't cook? Noah leveled his round eyes on her, all seriousness. "I know you want to argue, but imagine what will happen if Nestle Bingham bites into a big old ball of bandaid or bloody gauze." He pointed his forefinger at her. "You are not to touch any food, do you understand? You can oversee, that's all."

Manuel smiled confidently at her. "We'll make it work, Chef. I promise."

They were right. Bella would have to be okay with supervising. She had no choice. Maybe, at least, she could do something to fix non-cooking problems.

She looked at Noah and asked miserably, "What about this china Mason found?"

Within the hour she was sitting in the passenger seat of Eddie's car while Mason drove them out to his mother's house in Brooklyn to pick up boxes of china for Georgina's wedding.

"Does it hurt?" he asked, nodding at her bandaged thumb.

"Just my pride," she quipped.

He chuckled and some of the awkwardness between them dissipated. Bella had not intended for them to be awkward together, but then, she hadn't intended to spend any time with him either. Nothing like a long drive through New York traffic to give them ample time for uncomfortable moments.

There hadn't been any other option. Mason couldn't bring all of his mother's china back for them to go through, apparently she had quite the collection. It also wasn't fair to ask him to go alone and pick it out. Charlotte was too busy decorating and Bella was on pause since cutting her thumb.

Buckled in next to Mason as he drove, her injured thumb throbbing, her pride crumbling, her mind racing with all that needed to get done perfectly, Bella was having a hard time keeping herself together.

Tomorrow was Christmas Eve. Everything had to be ready

by then for the next day. She glanced over at Mason who was uncharacteristically quiet. He and Eddie had to be feeling the pinch, too.

"How are the plans going for your Christmas dinner?" Bella asked.

Mason had one hand wrapped around the top of the steering wheel as he maneuvered smoothly through traffic. His hand and wrist flexed as he drove, Bella noticed. It was distracting. She turned her gaze forward to look at the cars in front of them as she listened to his answer.

"It's going pretty good. We've got the first load of turkeys and hams. We're gonna do those tomorrow and warm them up with the sides on Christmas Day. That way we can do another round Christmas Day and serve twice the people."

"That's great," Bella said. She gave him a sideways look and smiled politely. "It's a very nice thing you and Eddie are doing."

"Yeah, we're really nice guys," he said with a touch of sarcasm. He cleared his throat, ready to change the subject. "So...about my Mom..."

Bella had to look at him. "What about your Mom?"

He shifted in his seat uncomfortably. "She can be...she's a little..."

Bella waited, amused. When he didn't continue, she asked, "She's a little...what?"

"Pushy," he said quickly. "She can be a little pushy."

"Oh, okay."

There was a long pause while Bella tried to think of what to say. Nothing came to mind.

Finally, Mason added, "I don't want you to think that I told her that we were...that we're..."

"That we're...what?"

"That we're dating," he blurted out. "She's going to assume it. That's all. I just wanted to warn you."

"Oh," she wanted to laugh, but he was already so worried, laughing probably wouldn't help.

"I don't usually bring girls home, that's all. She has high hopes, you know, for grandkids." Mason shut his mouth tight after letting that slip.

Bella bit her lip and managed a calm, "Thank you for warning me."

He looked at her sideways, adding, "I didn't want you to think I told her anything like that."

"Noted."

There was another long pause as he looked for an opening to get in the left lane to turn. When that was done he spoke again, but it was almost like he was talking to himself, "My Mom can be a lot, that's all."

Five minutes into meeting Mrs. Povich, Bella knew Mason had not been exaggerating.

"You sit here, Bella, I'll get you some coffee," Mrs. Povich insisted. She continued talking without allowing Bella to respond as she disappeared into the kitchen. "It's awful you cut your hand. Did you see a doctor? You look thin. How can a chef be thin? I'll bring you some cookies."

Bella waited obediently on the small floral loveseat with soft fat pillows, not sure they really had time for coffee and cookies.

Mason's tall frame seemed even larger in the cramped living room. In addition to the floral loveseat there were two reclining chairs in the same print, a large flat screen TV on one wall flanked by ceiling high book shelves, a glass topped oval coffee table that took up most of the walking area in the center of the room, a rug with a clashing floral pattern on the floor, two glass front china hutches on one wall and another corner china hutch wedged into the space next to the loveseat– three in all. Every nook and cranny was filled to overflowing with glass knick-knacks, vases full of silk flowers, or decorative plates sitting upright on little plastic stands. Everything in the room was bright and fluffy, even Mrs. Povich.

"I got most of it packed up for you two," Mrs. Povich's voice traveled out of the kitchen into the living room. "But Mason wouldn't tell me who's getting married?"

Mason shifted uncomfortably from one foot to the other as his mother brought out a tray full of coffee and a plate of butter cookies. Miraculously, she found a place to put it on the crowded coffee table in front of Bella and poured them each a cup of coffee as she held up her side of the one sided conversation.

"I think it must be somebody famous, because you had that TV show and probably know all kinds of famous people. Is that why it's hush hush? Because someone famous is getting married at your restaurant?" Mrs. Povich paused for a split second and Bella thought she might have a moment to answer, but no. "Do you take sugar or cream in your coffee, dear?" Bella shook her head 'no' and Mrs. Povich gave Mason a knowing look. He seemed embarrassed again, but Bella could not fathom why. "Here, have a few cookies with that. You need your energy what with all the happenings going on." She picked up the plate of cookies and raised them to Bella's nose. "I've never understood a chef that is too thin. It must be that you're working too hard." She gave Mason a sharp look as if it was his fault Bella was working too hard and was subsequently suffering from malnutrition.

Bella took a cookie and bit into it, hoping to oblige his mother, who was not a woman one would categorize as too thin and obviously felt strongly about keeping everyone well fed. The cookie was delicious, melting in her mouth with buttery sweetness.

"Will you be coming to church with Mason on Christmas Eve?"

Bella choked a little as she swallowed. "Um, no, unfortunately I can't make it. I'm working."

"Ma," Mason complained under his breath.

Mrs. Povich frowned at him. "What? I can't ask a few questions?" She turned back to Bella, her round face earnest with concern. "You're working on Christmas Eve and on Christmas Day?" She looked at Mason for an answer. When he didn't offer one, Mrs. Povich looked back to Bella and put a soft warm hand on hers. "Dear, you can't work all the time. It's not good for you. No wonder you hurt yourself. No wonder you're so thin. It won't be easy for you to have children if you stay so thin."

"Ma," Mason interrupted, his cheeks reddening. "Jeez, Ma–"

"Don't curse, Mason," Mrs. Povich reprimanded him.

Bella suppressed a smile. Watching Mason, a powerful, full grown man, squirm while his mother scolded him struck her as funny. The whole situation was funny.

"Where are the dishes?" Mason asked, hoping to steer the conversation in a new direction no doubt.

"I've got them in the den." Mrs. Povich patted Bella's hand again. "You take whatever you need for your celebrity wedding. I'm happy to help."

Soon they had ten boxes of china packed into Eddie's car and were headed out of Brooklyn. Bella had chosen six patterns out of the twelve Mrs. Povich owned for Charlotte to use for the wedding. Bella couldn't believe anyone owned twelve sets of china. She was still thinking about the little house stuffed full of pretty things when Mason cleared his throat to speak.

"Sorry about all of that," he said, glancing at her apologetically. "My Mom, she's incorrigible."

"It's okay. She's a mom."

They drove in silence for a while and Bella thought about

her mother. A pang of nostalgia made her feel a little sad. She needed to call her mother and check in. She'd been so busy lately she couldn't remember the last time she talked to her.

"Have any second thoughts about coming to church with me tomorrow?" Mason ventured with an almost nervous chuckle.

Bella stiffened. Her stomach tightened. She tried to smile and shrug his question off, but the tension in the car was suddenly palpable. He glanced at her, noticing something was wrong.

"Sorry, I–" he started.

"No, it's okay. I just can't think about anything besides the restaurant. I'm preoccupied."

An angsty quiet fell over them and Bella looked out the passenger window, pretending to watch the scenery.

"I shouldn't have said that. It was...pushy," Mason said as he stared straight ahead.

Bella didn't answer. She looked down at her lap where her bandaged hand was still throbbing and wished their trip was over. She would feel better once she was back at Total.

CHAPTER 22

Christmas Eve finally arrived.

The anticipation was so intense Bella was almost ill. She had tossed and turned all night, too, blaming it on the cut on her hand or the events looming in front of her instead of the uncomfortable ending to her excursion with Mason.

In truth, she couldn't pinpoint what was keeping her awake. There were so many options to choose from. At four in the morning she gave up the pretense of laying in bed and decided to shower and get ready for the day.

Dressing and doing her hair took longer than normal because of her bandaged hand and she tried not to dwell on her stupid mistake with the knife. Maybe it would turn out better to be overseeing instead of hands on cooking.

"Right," she muttered, not quite believing her own positive self-talk.

Bella looked at her reflection in the full length mirror. Black slacks, white shirt, her dark hair pulled back into a long braid. Despite the bandages, she had managed to put herself together fairly well.

She frowned at her wounded hand. Putting it behind her back she stood up straight and practiced a mock greeting. Maybe rehearsing everything in her head would help her nerves.

"Hello, Mr. Bingham. Hello Rosamonde, how wonderful to see you. Thank you both for coming." She sighed. She could probably rehearse all day and night and still be nervous tomorrow at the party. The sound of her cell phone ringing pulled her away from the mirror and when she picked it up she was glad to see it was her mother.

"Hola, Mama," Bella answered. They continued their conversation in Spanish as Bella put on her winter coat and hat and took off walking to Total. As she made her way through the freezing pre-dawn morning, she answered her mother's questions.

No, she had not made a Roscon de Reyes.

No, she didn't have any dinner plans except for whatever they were serving at the restaurant.

No, she wasn't going to Christmas Eve mass.

By the time she arrived at Total, Bella felt like the worst daughter in the world. She had moved across the ocean to America. She was a workaholic. She wasn't married and there were no grandchildren on the horizon. All of her life choices, it seemed, were turning out to be a big disappointment to her mother.

Luckily, Posie and several others were already in the kitchen receiving deliveries and preparing for their regular customers as well as the events coming up tomorrow. Bella had little time to think about her failings as a daughter. The time had come to stop worrying and dive into the work at hand.

Smooth Christmas music played throughout the whole restaurant, delicious smells filled the air, and everyone was full of the Christmas spirit.

"You should take a look at the third floor," Noah told her when she stepped out of the kitchen for a break. "Charlotte has pulled off a miracle."

Bella poured some cinnamon spice tea in a teapot, put it on a tray with a few cups and some of Posie's Christmas cookies, and carried the tray carefully up to the third floor. When she pushed open the double doors she stopped to take in the decor. Charlotte—and Davis—really had pulled off a miracle.

The original hardwood floors were refinished in a dark stain that matched the window frames. The tall, arched windows were sparkling clean and draped with boughs of evergreen that had been wrapped in white lights and decorated with bunches of red cranberries and shimmering red and black Christmas bulbs. The wedding alter was a literal arbor covered in a thick layer of red roses, shining black ribbon, and baby's breath interlaced with the same little white lights.

"What do you think?" Charlotte asked happily.

"Wow, Charlie, this is beautiful. You've really done an excellent job," Bella handed her friend a cup of tea.

"Well, I had some great helpers," Charlotte nodded towards a woman and a man that Bella didn't know. "Kelly and Mark are super talented and they live in the city. They would be great to bring on board for future events."

Bella offered Kelly and Mark some tea, which they accepted graciously as Charlotte introduced Bella as the owner of Total.

"We really appreciate this opportunity," Kelly gushed.

"Yes, Ms. Velez, thank you for this job. We've been out of work for a while," Mark added.

Bella understood they were referred by Mason to help over the busy days and was reminded of his generous spirit even as she was reminded of her own self-centeredness. Not only was she a disappointment as a daughter, she was a Scrooge of a boss. Worried about the wild success of her restaurant at this time of year when other people were struggling to put food on the table. Shameful.

"No, thank *you*," Bella said gratefully, taking in the beautifully decorated room. "This looks amazing. It's going to be an outstanding wedding." She looked back to them, wanting to connect a little more on their mutual acquaintance with Mason. "Will you be having Christmas Dinner at Pits? They've been cooking for days. Probably have enough food to have dinner tonight and tomorrow if they wanted to."

Mark nodded jovially. "We'll have to wait until tomorrow. They're closed tonight."

Bella was surprised. She had expected them to stay open like normal, right alongside Total, all evening.

"Christmas Eve," Kelly added, as if that explained everything.

It did explain everything. Bella knew immediately what Mason was doing. Letting all of his staff off the night before Christmas because they would be working on Christmas Day was a thoughtful and kind gesture.

She frowned. Why hadn't she thought of that?

"How's your hand?" Charlotte asked.

"It's not too bad," Bella answered distractedly.

"Can you cook?" Charlotte asked.

"No, it's too fresh. I'm relegated to supervising...unfortunately."

Charlotte, always the optimist, giggled and said quietly, "You have years of experience whispering instructions to me on camera. You should be fine."

Bella wanted to laugh, but had been overcome with the realization of her own miserly tendencies. Everyone at Total had been working so hard and she was expecting them to keep serving dinner on Christmas Eve to a small crowd of patrons? Christmas Eve was a night for families. They didn't have a large dinner rush on any night, why should she expect it on Christmas Eve?

"We're closing at five," she blurted out. Charlotte and the other two gave her a queer look. "Too...I mean, we're closing at five *also*. For Christmas Eve."

"Oh...great!" Charlotte was genuinely delighted.

Bella cringed with guilt about that, too. She had let her own troubles overtake her friend's vacation. Charlotte had been working since she arrived in New York.

"In fact, I need to go help Noah wrap some things up before five," Bella announced, turning on her heel to hurry downstairs and inform Noah and the rest of her staff that they were going to spend Christmas Eve with their families.

Joy fluttered through her heart at the thought, pushing all of her other worries out of her mind. Who would have thought that copying Mason's generosity could put her more in the Christmas spirit than anything.

Just as Bella reached the door to the stairway, Charlotte called out after her, "Bella, if you're not working tonight that means you can come to Christmas Eve mass with us!"

CHAPTER 23

"We got such good seats!" Charlotte exclaimed happily as she leaned back in the pew and looked around at the grandeur of St. Agnus Cathedral.

Bella's head was still spinning after the whirlwind closing of Total for the night, the rush to get changed for Christmas Eve mass, and the race to get to Brooklyn in time to get a seat, let alone a good seat.

She managed a smile as she took note of their position, just left of center and only ten rows back from the altar. "Very good seats," she agreed.

Candlelight flickered against the shining wooden alter that rose up in front of hand carved wooden pews, enough to fit hundreds of people on a normal Sunday, all creaking under the weight of the extra guests in the Christmas Eve mass crowd. The white stone walls of the old cathedral stretched four stories high behind the alter, peaking at the center point and providing a magnificent backdrop to whoever was speaking to the congregation. Wide steps covered in red carpet filled the space behind the alter. Bella expected the choir would stand there during mass.

Anticipation squeezed her stomach. She wasn't sure how to feel about watching Mason, a grown man, sing in a church choir, yet she couldn't deny a tiny thrill at the idea of seeing him. Conflicted, she fiddled with the small white candle she had been handed when she walked in.

Everything about this excursion was giving Bella mixed feelings. As they had hurried through the frosty night, Davis escorting both of them carefully to make sure they didn't stumble in their high heels, she was filled with excitement. The fun of being dressed up and out with friends, the beauty of the great stone cathedral surrounded by an ornate iron fence, people streaming from all directions up the stairs and into the tall gothic doors, all reminded her that this was a special night. A night that was celebrated all around the world.

Another part of her, however, was sick with nerves. For not only were they attending Christmas Eve mass, they were attending Mason's church at his invitation. Bella could barely allow that fact to enter her mind without trembling.

"Are you cold?" Davis asked. He was peering at her around Charlotte who sat between them and must have misinterpreted her nerves for shivering.

"Should you go get her coat?" Charlotte asked him, concerned.

"No, no," Bella held up her palm to stop him. He had been such a gentleman to take their coats, push against the crowd to get them to the massive coat rack and find a spot to hang them up, she didn't want him to bother with trying to retrieve hers. Besides, she wasn't cold. She was agitated. She smiled reassuringly at Charlotte, "I'm not cold, I promise."

Satisfied, Charlotte snuggled back into the pew, Davis' arm draped over her shoulders. A pang of melancholy touched Bella's heart and she looked away and tried to focus on the beauty of the grand cathedral instead of her own wild emotional swings.

When it felt as if the worship space was nearly bursting with people, all dressed in their best, each clutching their own small white candle, chattering and laughing, full of the Christmas spirit, a side door behind the altar opened and the choir filed in, filling the wide steps.

Bella was surprised to see all of the women dressed in floor length black dresses and the men in tuxedos. But maybe that was to be expected. After all, she had worn her best red dress and the rest of the congregation was equally well turned out, why wouldn't the choir be in formal attire?

She took a deep breath, ready to control her reaction when she finally saw Mason. She didn't want Charlotte to get any ideas about her and Mason dating again. She just wanted to get through this evening and have as nice a time as possible before the big day tomorrow. But when he finally appeared, ducking a little to get through the small side door without bumping his head, Bella's breath caught in her throat.

Mason's tall fit frame was even more becoming donning a tuxedo. He stood a few inches above every other man in the choir, but not in an awkward towering way, more in an ultra-masculine way. He dominated not only with his height, but with his good looks. In place of his normal easy smile was an appropriately composed expression for the occasion, which did nothing to diminish his appeal. His sandy blonde hair remained the same as always, though, tousled and sexy, sending a tingle of attraction through Bella.

She gripped her little white candle harder and felt Char-lotte watching her reaction. Just when she thought she would have to turn to her friend and explain that she was definitely not affected by Mason being gorgeous in his tuxedo, Bella was saved the trouble. The choir was in place and the organ music began, kicking off the ceremony.

When the choir began their first song, Hark the Herald Angels Sing, complete with trumpets announcing the arrival of Baby Jesus, Bella was impressed. The music raised the level of joy and reverence of the occasion, making it truly enjoyable.

Charlotte nudged her and leaned over to whisper in her ear, "He's looking for you."

Bella looked immediately to Mason and found him scanning the crowded sanctuary. Charlotte raised one hand just over the tops of their heads and waved. Bella wanted to sink into the floor.

"Stop," she whispered at Charlotte, but it was too late. Mason found them in the crowd, and locked eyes with Bella for a long moment.

Bella's didn't know if she should smile or wave or bow her head and ignore him. She smiled despite herself and one side of Mason's mouth raised in an almost smile as he sang. Then, quickly, before she had time to think about anything else, he winked at her and turned his attention back to the conductor.

Several women seated around them turned discreetly to look at her and she knew she wasn't the only one who had seen him wink. Bella's cheeks burned. She stared at the orchestral musicians who played along with the choir as if they were the most interesting orchestra she had ever seen. Without looking, she knew Charlotte had seen the wink, too.

Mass went on and on...and on, leaving plenty of time for everyone to forget about the wink.

Everyone except Bella.

Incensed that he had singled her out with a wink she tried to ignore him, tried to push down the feelings that rose in her heart. Pleasure. Elation. She bid her mind to focus on the reason for this church service and the joy that it represented for so many people around the world.

Yet no matter what she did, her thoughts kept turning back to his wink and her heart would not be soured against him.

His solo didn't help.

After the priest was done speaking and all of the prayers and songs had been sung, right as Bella thought they would be lighting their candles and singing Silent Night together, Mason stepped out in front of the choir. He straightened his tuxedo jacket and nodded to the conductor that he was ready. The music began, the simple yet beautiful intro to Ave Maria floated across the sanctuary.

"No way," Charlotte said under her breath.

As if in answer, Mason began the song, "Ave Maria...Gratia plena...Maria, gratia plena..."

Bella tore her eyes away from Mason for a moment to give Charlotte a look of shock. How could it be that the fun loving, ex-Army boxer, barbecue boy from Pits was singing Ave Maria as purely as Pavarotti himself?

Charlotte shook her head, impressed and speechless, for once.

Bella let the sound of Mason's pure voice wrap around her and pull at her soul. She could hardly believe what was happening. His voice was so powerful, so perfect, it held everyone in the room captive, not only her. But for Bella, the spell was even stronger. With every note it was as if Mason reached into her chest and grabbed hold of her heart.

When he finished, silence hung in the air. The moment was almost too holy to speak or even to move. Finally, the unexpected sound of applause erupted. Mason, who was stepping back into his place in the choir, ducked his head bashfully.

Bella couldn't explain or control her reaction. She wanted

to applaud, but remained frozen. She wanted to find his eyes and smile at him, let him see her reaction, but she couldn't do that either.

The rest of the service was a blur of praying, lighting candles, and singing. She went through the motions like someone watching from outside her own body. Her heart, mind, and soul still reverberating with Mason's performance of Ave Maria.

When everything was over and the congregation was released, Bella was warm. Too warm. There was hardly room to move as the whole body of people turned their attention to leaving the building. There was hardly room to breathe.

"I need to get some air," Bella told Charlotte and Davis as they moved with the throng towards the long coat racks.

"We'll get our coats and meet you out front," Charlotte said.

Bella made her way through the crowd and a continual flow of happy greetings. Calls of "Merry Christmas" surrounded her as she made her way to the door.

When she managed to step out onto the stone steps, it was snowing. Big, fat, frozen flakes pummeled down from above bringing even more Christmas joy to the church goers. Cold air hit her lungs as she took in a deep breath of relief.

"Thank goodness," she said out loud, though nobody seemed to be paying much attention to her as they went on their merry ways.

Bella went to the bottom of the steps and to the side to stay out of the flow of foot traffic and took in another deep breath. She wondered if she had been close to fainting inside the cathedral, the snow and cold felt so good. Overheated, that's what she'd been. Nothing else.

Bella took a few steps down the sidewalk. She was too agitated to stand still, but couldn't go far without Charlotte and Davis, so she paced carefully back and forth, trying to walk out her emotions.

It wasn't working. The wild sensations she had felt inside the sanctuary were repeating in a loop, rushing first through her mind then down through her heart and into the pit of her stomach before racing back up to her mind to start the process all over again. Mason had taken hold of her completely and no amount of cold or pacing, it seemed, could make him disappear.

"Bella!"

At first she thought she had imagined his voice calling out to her, that she had been so overcome by thoughts of him that her wishful thinking was making her hallucinate. But, no, as she whirled around in response to her name she saw him at the top of the steps.

Still in his tuxedo, but with the bow tie undone, Mason stood a head taller than everyone else streaming out of the doors. When he saw her see him, he lifted one arm and waved.

"Bella, wait!" he called out, stepping down onto the top step before throwing his leg over the railing and jumping easily to the ground.

Unable to tear her eyes away from the vision of him jogging towards her through the heavy flakes of snow, Bella stared mutely. She couldn't make a sound to greet him in response.

"Hi," Mason stopped in front of her, a little breathless, his eyes shining. "You...you look beautiful."

Bella glanced down at her red dress, fluffy white flakes of snow were scattered across the fabric. The snow was probably sticking in her hair, too, just like it was sticking in his. She looked up into his eyes. Her heart skipped a beat.

He smiled and cocked his head, "You kind of look like a Christmas angel."

Bella laughed and his smile widened. The snow fell down around them at a dizzying speed. Mesmerized by his gaze and the twinkle in his eyes, she reached out and touched the lapel of his jacket.

"You look nice, too," she said. Her fingers trembled as she touched him.

Mason frowned. "You're freezing. We need to get you inside."

She shook her head, another tremble moving through her whole body. "No, please, I don't want to go inside."

He paused, searching her eyes for a reason. Then, without another word, he took his tuxedo jacket off and threw it over her shoulders. The warmth of his body still in the lining, the jacket hung large on her smaller frame. She pulled it around her tightly while Mason led her underneath one of the large trees that lined the street, shielding them from the heavy snow.

"There," he said, peering out from under the snow covered branches towards the church before turning back to her. "Is that better?"

She nodded, a shiver moved across her skin. She clutched the jacket more tightly as Mason studied her carefully.

"What's the matter?" he asked.

"You were wonderful tonight," she said shakily.

Flattered, he tried to shrug off her compliment, but Bella could tell he was pleased.

"Oh, that. My Mom likes it when I sing."

"More people than just your Mom like it I think."

He dismissed the thought with a quick shake of his head and focused on her again, "That's not why you're out here in the snow without your coat, though, is it?"

Bella didn't know how to explain that his singing was exactly the reason why she was outside in the freezing snow without her coat. Something had happened when he sang. Something she didn't understand.

Seeing that she wasn't going to elaborate, Mason decided to change the subject. "I'm glad you came. Was the restaurant slow?"

"We closed...for Christmas Eve."

Mason nodded his approval. "That's good. Nobody should have to work on Christmas Eve."

A stab of guilt penetrated their magical moment in the snow, poking a hole in it and letting her all too familiar stress and anxiety seep in.

"Yes, well, I realized that I've gotten a little caught up in everything. Everybody has worked so hard..." Bella's voice trailed off. She looked down at her bright red high heels standing out against the fallen snow. Mason had worked harder than anybody over the last few weeks and he had still managed to stay in a good mood, sing in his church choir, and even remain humble while he stood around in his tuxedo looking like a male model.

"Bella..." he said.

She was brought back to the moment by the tone in his voice. There was something soft in it, sensual. "Yes?"

He shifted on his feet awkwardly, reminding her of his embarrassment at his mother's house, charming her all over again.

"Bella, I..."

Every time he said her name an electrical charge shimmied down her spine. She inched closer to him without even thinking.

"I know you've got a lot going on and you...you don't want to make any mistakes." Pain flashed across his face as he said it and Bella knew she had put that pain there. Her heart wrung with profound regret. A smile returned to his eyes as he gazed down at her, a twinkle of something like hope glimmering in them. "I didn't think you would come tonight, but you're here..."

Bella leaned towards him. The snow covered tree above and the cascade of snowflakes falling just outside of where they stood together made it feel like they were all alone in the world. Cocooned against reality, it felt like anything was possible.

"Mason..." she said, his name whispering out of her soul.

Something more than a twinkle flashed in his eyes and he moved closer. Bella could have reached up and tied his bow tie. Instead she let her gaze linger on the top three buttons he had unbuttoned, leaving the center of his neck exposed. He swallowed hard and she lifted her eyes to his, inviting him. Desire filled her body and all she wanted was his kiss.

He started to speak again, but the words caught in his throat. He raised his hand to the side of her face and pushed a tendril of snow covered hair back from her temple. Bella shivered. He traced the tip of his finger down her cheek and along her jaw to her chin. She shivered again as he lifted her chin up towards him. He leaned down to kiss her.

Bella's stomach tightened. She was gripped with fear. Just as his lips were about to press onto hers, she raised both of her hands and put her palms on his chest, pushing him away.

"Wait," she said, breathless but firm.

He stopped, confusion replacing the passion in his eyes.

"No," she said. "I can't..."

He stepped back. "No?"

Bella couldn't explain. There was no explanation that would make sense, she knew that. She watched him move away from her, pleading wordlessly with her eyes.

"Bella," he said softly, almost sadly. "I have to tell you. I think I might be falling in love with you."

The magic of their moment waned and the icy cold of the night pressed in on her.

Silence. Frozen quiet. Bella stared up at him, disbelief filling her heart and chilling her bones.

"Falling in love with me?" The words left her mouth laced with scorn and they hit Mason right in the heart, she could see the pain in his eyes.

"I see that's not what you want to hear."

Confusion and surprise filled her and she stammered an answer, "I don't…I can't, Mason…I have so many things to do. So many things going on. I can't be in love."

He shook his head, stepping back from her and turning so all she could see was his profile. Coughing out a laugh, he ran his hand through his hair. "Right, right…you can't make any mistakes."

"Don't be like this, Mason, please…I can't…it's just one too many things to worry about."

He turned back to her, but all of his sweet sexiness was gone, replaced with hurt and disappointment. "Love isn't just a thing, Bella. It's *the* thing. What do we have in all of this if we don't have love?"

She opened her mouth to answer, but couldn't think of an answer. She reached out towards him. "I'm sorry."

He moved just far enough away that she couldn't touch him and dropped his eyes to the ground. "Don't be sorry. Forget about it."

Bella cringed at his words. Everything was wrong. She had ruined everything…again.

"Bella!" Charlotte's voice rang out from the nearby steps. She and Davis were making their way down, Davis holding onto Charlotte with one hand and carrying Bella's coat in the other.

"Davis has my coat," Bella said, slipping Mason's jacket off and holding it out to him. "Thank you."

He took it without looking her in the eye. Instead of

putting it on, he stepped out from under the tree into the snow.

"Mason," she said, wishing he wouldn't go.

He looked back at her once, his eyes dark green, and said, "Merry Christmas, Bella." Then he was gone.

CHAPTER 24

Christmas morning hit Bella with a flurry of activity. There wasn't a single solitary second where she wasn't consumed with organizing for the party or a minute that went by without having to double check something for the wedding. All morning, not a moment of her time could be spared to relive what Mason had said under the snowy tree, which suited her mood. She would rather be busy than rethink her response.

While the rest of the world slept in and spent time with their families opening gifts under their Christmas trees, Bella and the others chopped and sliced, braised and simmered, tasted and perfected for each dish being served that day. Bella was still designated too injured to touch anything, but she had plenty to do with overseeing.

More than a few times the smell of smoking turkey and ham came to her from the back alley. She imagined Mason and Eddie laughing and cooking and getting ready for their big charity event and she was tempted to peek out the back door to take a look. She didn't. It would be too awkward...and she was afraid the sight of him would bring back the heartache that had kept her awake half the night.

"Georgina's mother is going to be here in a little bit," Charlotte poked her head into the kitchen to warn everyone.

"Don't let her back to see the cake until I tell you!" Posie's voice rose up over the other kitchen noises from the walk in cooler where she was putting final touches on her edible poinsettias.

"Okay," Charlotte called back, her eyes twinkling with amusement. "Do you want to see what just happened?" she asked Bella directly.

Bella's stomach dropped. "Now what?"

"Just come and see," Charlotte insisted.

Filled with dread, Bella followed her out into Total's dining room where, to her astonishment, she saw a tall, bushy Christmas tree covered in hundreds of blinking white lights put up in the corner next to the window.

Noah stood next to it rearranging some of the lights. When he saw Bella he gestured towards the tree like a game show host and said, "Ta-da!"

Delighted at the giant tree, and more than a little relieved the surprise was good news, Bella asked, "Where did that come from?"

"Mason and Eddie brought it over a little bit ago," Charlotte beamed at Bella as she told the story. "They didn't want us to disturb you in the kitchen."

"Oh..." Bella's good reaction faded.

"Mason said they ordered two for Pits, but only one would fit," Noah added.

Charlotte gave Bella a knowing look. "I think he ordered an extra one for you on purpose."

"Me, too," Noah agreed. He and Charlotte shared a look.

"I'm sure he didn't," Bella answered, but she knew they were right.

The tree was too big for the corner, its fat branches were packed with fragrant needles that intruded on the tables nearest to them. Noah was busy rearranging the seating at those tables to make it less cramped.

"It's kind of big, but it adds, doesn't it?" Charlotte voiced exactly what Bella was thinking.

"It does make the room feel...merrier," Bella said.

"Exactly! More homey," Noah agreed, putting the final chair in place.

They all stepped back and admired the tree. Bella couldn't help but think of how much it was like Mason. Too tall, last minute, twinkly, bright, a little out of place, but somehow making her feel warm and happy. She thought about his mother's little living room chock full of knick knacks and floral prints and smiled.

"Do you feel like talking about what happened last night yet?" Charlotte asked her quietly.

Bella had refused to go into any details on the way back from Christmas Eve mass, even though Charlotte had been dying to know. She had hardly wanted to go into how she had refused Mason's attempt at romancing her, and how it had left her with a hollow pit in her stomach.

She squirmed a little under her friend's renewed curiosity, choosing to stare intently at their new Christmas tree instead.

Charlotte watched her and was about to say something else when Georgina's mother, wrapped in a black fur with a matching black fur hat, appeared in Total's front picture window. She strode to the front door and flung it open like some kind of Russian oligarch's wife. The sleigh bells on the door rang loudly.

Bella gave Charlotte a sly look and said, "Saved by the jingle bells."

Manuel stuck his head out of the kitchen. "Chef, do you want to taste the citrus chocolate glaze?"

"Yes, I'm coming," Bella hurried back to the kitchen, her haven, before Charlotte could ask her anything else and before she got sucked into a pre-tour of the wedding decor with Georgina's mother.

Relieved to be surrounded by stainless steel and the sweet and savory smells of Total's kitchen, Bella determined to stay hidden there as long as she possibly could. She didn't want to talk about Mason with Charlotte, she didn't want to accidentally run into him, and she didn't want to face any last minute problems.

"If one more thing goes wrong," she muttered to herself.

"What was that?" Manuel asked, his close attention to detail included listening to everything she said.

"Nothing," she answered. She dipped the tip of a spoon into the glaze he was working on, tasting it with pleasure. The tang of orange zest combined with the rich chocolate with just the right amount of sweetness. "Perfect, Manuel. Perfect."

Bella didn't emerge from the kitchen until well into what would normally be their lunch rush. Since it was Christmas Day, however, the normal steady stream of customers was non-existent, so Bella told the staff they should eat their lunch in the dining room.

"Pits packed up some turkey and ham for us," Davis announced as he carried two plastic bags full of to-go containers through the front door. "They're really hopping over there."

"Mmm," Noah took the containers from Davis. "We'll have our own Christmas dinner right now."

Bella went to the front window next to the new Christmas tree and looked out. Dozens and dozens of people were waiting in the fresh snow right outside Total to get into

Pits for their free Christmas meal. The line extended far longer than she could see and was made up of a variety of people. Young and old, single people, couples, and families, all in high spirits even though they were standing out in the cold.

She glanced up at the giant tree Mason had brought them, then over to the Christmas Spider that still glittered happily above their cash register.

"Are you going to have some lunch?" Charlotte asked. She and Davis were gathered with Noah and the staff around a few of the tables, which they had strewn with some Christmas dinner delectables, including Mason's turkey and ham.

"Yes, you all go ahead," Bella smiled at them. They had all worked so hard and everything was right on time for the party and the wedding. A feeling of satisfaction warmed her and she thought about how much Mason had helped this past month. How much he always seemed to put his heart into everything he did.

She turned back to look at the line of people waiting outside of Pits and noticed three older men sitting on a stoop across the street. All three were eating from styrofoam containers, steam rising from their complimentary Christmas dinners into the freezing winter air.

Bella frowned.

"Pits doesn't have enough seating inside for the crowd that's showing up," Davis said. He had moved up next to her, holding a plate piled with ham, cornbread stuffing, and a homemade roll. His gaze rested on the same three men Bella was watching. "I guess not everybody has a place to take their takeout."

Bella's frown deepened. How many people were going to be forced to eat their Christmas dinner out on the street? She looked back at Total's empty dining room. So elegant. Cool

Christmas jazz playing over the speakers, tables draped in pristine white tablecloths and set with tasteful red candles surrounded by fresh pine wreaths, everything perfectly prepared for their upcoming events.

"I'll be right back," she said abruptly. Without grabbing her jacket, Bella pushed open the front door with a jingle and made her way through the crowd to Pits' front door.

"Excuse me, sorry, I just need to get inside to speak to the owner," she apologized to those waiting in line.

Warm air filled with the smell of smoked meat and freshly baked bread wrapped around her as she stepped inside. Elvis belted out, "It's Christmas time pretty baby, the snow is falling on the ground." Even though the music was loud, the din from the diners was even louder. All of Pits small tables were packed with people enjoying their meal and the rest of the floor was packed with people waiting patiently for their food, so packed Bella couldn't see who was working the counter.

A fat Christmas tree that matched Total's was crammed into the far back corner of the room, it was covered in bright red, green, blue and purple lights that blinked off and on. Tinsel garland in the same bright colors hung anywhere and everywhere garland could hang. Though she didn't see any Christmas Spiders anywhere, Pits' ambience reflected its owners—fun, joyful, full of energy. It was like she had walked into a jolly elf after party, kegs of ale and all.

"Got no sleigh with reindeer, no sack on my back..." Mason's voice rang out above the noise, singing along with Elvis and knocking everyone's socks off with its power.

She stood on tip toe and could just see the tops of two Santa hats moving around behind the counter. A sparkle of anticipation filled her heart and she pressed forward.

"Bella! Merry Christmas," Eddie called out when she managed to slip up to the side of the counter.

"Hi, Eddie," she returned his wide smile. "Merry Christmas to you, too."

Mason, who was handing a bag with three styrofoam containers to a middle aged couple on the other side of the counter, didn't turn to greet her right away. The short, round woman standing next to him did.

"Hello, Bella, so nice to see you again," Mrs. Povich smiled warmly. She wore her own Santa hat and a long sleeved T-shirt with a cartoon image of a reindeer and the word Prancer printed underneath. Her cheeks were as red as apples.

"Hi, Bella," Mavis, Mason's sister from the ice skating rink, squeezed behind him and came to greet her. She, too, wore a Santa hat and a T-shirt that matched her mother's, except hers was named Vixen.

Surprised at the sight of them and suddenly feeling naked without a crazy red Santa hat and reindeer T-shirt, Bella said, "Merry Christmas."

"Is everything all right?" Mason had finally turned his attention to her from the far end of the counter, but his greeting was less than jolly. It certainly didn't match the funny faced reindeer named Dasher on his T-shirt.

Bella kept smiling, though the sparkle in her heart was fizzling fast at his lack of enthusiasm.

"No, no, everything's fine," she said quickly.

"You came for some turkey?" Eddie asked, holding up a container. Bella noted his reindeer was named Dancer.

"No, no, we're eating what you already sent over. It's delicious," she said, though she hadn't tasted a bite.

Mason continued to watch her, waiting for an explanation. Tongue-tied, she couldn't quite recall her reason for interrupting the good times going on in the little barbecue place. All she could see was that Mason's eyes weren't twinkling at her like they always did, he was stiff and uncomfortable, standing quietly behind the others, not moving, not smiling.

Bella's heart sank.

She had grown so used to his smile. Grown used to the way he lit up the room—lit up her heart—when he smiled. She loved his smile. She hadn't realized how much she relied on seeing it when he was around.

"I–I wanted to tell you that our dining room is empty," she said, remembering her errand in a rush.

They all waited for more of an explanation, not understanding what she was offering.

Bella swung her hand towards the people packed into Pits standing shoulder to shoulder. "I thought you could send people there to eat their Christmas dinner since you're overflowing."

"That's great, Bella!" Eddie declared with his deep laugh.

Bella backed away from the counter, wanting to escape any further depressing interaction with Mason. "Just tell anyone to come over if they want to eat their dinner while it's hot," she said.

"We will!" Mrs. Povich answered happily. She glanced back and up at her son, who had yet to respond.

"Thanks, that's nice of you," Mason said politely.

Bella blushed in a rush of embarrassment that didn't make sense to anyone except Mason. "It's the least I can do, really, after everything you've done," she said rapidly before turning on her heel and pushing back out the door.

As she hurried through the icy cold to invite the three older men dining outside to come into her restaurant to eat, she knew what she had said was true. Offering Total for Mason and Eddie to use for their charity event was the absolute least she could have done.

CHAPTER 25

Soon Total's dining room was full of people enjoying their takeout Christmas dinners. Strangers struck up conversations, waiters and cooks mingled with the guests, and the whole room took on an easy, festive feeling. Much more festive than when it had simply been a pristine empty space waiting for a party.

"This is fun," Posie said after having a merry visit with a young couple and their new baby. Posie's spiky red hair often became a focal point for little children, and her fun personality almost always made little ones giggle. "It's almost like we're breaking in the room for the bigger party later, don't you think?"

Bella nodded. She had thought that herself as she watched the staff relax into the vibe of the Pits patrons. "It is nice," Bella agreed. "It didn't seem right to make people eat outside in the cold." She didn't mention how she thought Mason's natural generosity might be rubbing off on her, even though there was no more possibility of romance.

Posie gave her a good natured nudge. "I'm glad you're

getting into the spirit of the season, Bella. You've been awfully tense."

"Bella!" Kelly, from the Mark and Kelly duo who helped Charlotte set up for the wedding, waved at her from one of the tables.

Bella greeted them warmly, happy to see them enjoying a good meal in the fine dining room.

"You have such a beautiful restaurant," Kelly gushed. "We hope to come back when the holidays are over and eat here." Something in the way Mark shifted in his chair at her comment caught Bella's attention. He lowered his eyes, obviously uncomfortable and Bella suddenly realized why. They were both out of work and eating a free Christmas dinner, maybe they wouldn't be able to afford to eat at Total in the near future. Or ever.

A pang of concern for them and everyone else who had gone to Pits for food struck Bella's heart. She had an overwhelming urge to reassure them, to do something to help.

"I'm hoping tonight's wedding will put us on the map for more weddings...which would mean we would need more help from you two," she said.

Kelly's eyes brightened and Mark lifted his gaze. "Really?" he asked.

Bella nodded, hoping more than ever that she could book tons of weddings and hire them. "Of course! Charlotte can't stop talking about what a great job you two did. And employees get a fifty percent discount at Total," she announced. She would have to let Noah in on the new policy, but it felt like the right thing to do. A genuine smile on her lips, she realized she might be catching on to the whole Christmas spirit thing.

As the pre-party went on, Bella's heart warmed. Many of the diners from Pits stayed on and helped clean up after themselves. Some of them had already been hired by Total to assist with the evening's events. And some of them had a natural knack for making the room feel merrier.

Bella didn't feel the need to draw an imaginary line between this naturally occurring party and the one she had planned to begin at six o'clock. Besides the hustle and bustle helped her nerves. As the band arrived for the reception upstairs and the florist made their final delivery under Charlotte's watchful eye, everything felt like it was coming together seamlessly.

Right after five, Charlotte let her know, "Georgina is going to be here any minute. Her and the wedding party are going upstairs to get settled in."

"Right!" Bella's eyes flew open, she had rather lost track of time.

"Don't panic, I've got it under control. I just wanted to remind you."

"I should get in the kitchen and—" Bella was cut off mid-sentence by the epic whirlwind that was Georgina in a gigantic crystal encrusted wedding gown emerging from a sleek black limousine that had just pulled up outside. Flanked by her mother, who wore a deep red evening gown, and three other women in black evening gowns with plunging neck-lines—the bridesmaids no doubt—Georgina moved towards Total's front door. She towered over the others with the graceful determination of an ice queen on her way to reside over court.

"Oh my," Charlotte said with a chuckle. She stepped towards the door to usher the bridal party in and looked over her shoulder at Bella, "Wish me luck!"

Bella held her breath as Charlotte led Georgina past all of the not so well dressed merry makers in the dining room, but nothing seemed to phase the bride. She didn't even look in Bella's direction. Neither did the groom and his entourage who arrived several minutes later in their own limousine.

R.C. Reynolds, Georgina's betrothed, was smaller than expected, but he had a powerful presence, the kind that comes from possessing extreme wealth. Short, black hair, greying at the temples, and a well cut tuxedo improved his appeal despite his smaller stature. Tuxedos always made men more attractive.

Bella's mind slipped back to Mason in his tuxedo and her stomach did another flip-flop. "Stop it," she whispered, willing the memory to disappear.

"Chef?" Manuel was standing at her elbow. "Shall I move to Pits' kitchen?"

"Yes, yes, it's time," Bella agreed, another twinge of regret pinching her heart at the mention of Mason's place.

She caught Noah's attention as he showed Georgina's future husband and company the stairway. Bella mouthed *I'm going to the kitchen* and Noah nodded in understanding. Bella hurried towards her sanctuary. It was time to cook up a storm and she was glad for the distraction.

Just as she placed her hand on the heavy swinging door, Bella heard, "Oh, there you are!"

She turned to find Mason's mother, still in her Prancer T-shirt, smiling at her excitedly. "I saw your celebrity bride arrive!"

Surprised and slightly confused, it took Bella a moment to realize she was speaking about Georgina. "Yes, she did. They're all upstairs now. But I don't know if she is really much of a celebrity." Mrs. Povich's face fell. "I think she's pretty wealthy though, so...maybe?" Bella added, not sure how to address Mason's mother's disappointment.

The little lady's face brightened. She patted Bella on the arm. "You have a beautiful place, dear. Do you mind if I look around?"

Bella glanced at the pre-party that would soon morph into the actual Christmas party with previously invited guests. "Of course, stay as long as you like. The party is just beginning."

Mrs. Povich beamed. "Thank you, dear."

"You're welcome," Bella replied before escaping into the kitchen.

It only took a few minutes to forget about her interaction with Mrs. Povich. The kitchen was hopping and since she couldn't touch any of the food with her injured hand, Bella kept an eye on what each and every one of her people were mixing, stirring, braising, frying, roasting and baking.

Bella forgot about the wedding going on upstairs. She forgot about the Christmas party guests arriving. Lost in the sights and smells of every tasty bite of food arranged beautifully on its tray as the waiters carried them out the swinging doors, she only felt a glimmer of regret about Mason reverberating through her heart. With enough time and work Bella hoped that glimmer would fade away completely.

Noah stuck his head into the kitchen and caught her eye. "He's here," he said firmly.

Bella froze. Her heart leapt into her chest. She tried to sound nonchalant, "Mason?"

Confusion flitted through Noah's eyes and he shook his head, correcting her in a stage whisper, "No, Nestle Bingham!"

Her heart crashed mid-flight and dropped into her stomach. "With Rosamonde?"

Noah nodded dramatically, "Yes, both of them."

Bella took in a deep breath. Everything was going to be all right. She willed it to be so. All of the food leaving the kitchen had been perfect. She had nothing to be nervous about.

"I'll be out in a minute," she glanced around the busy kitchen. She would double check everything in the kitchen to stall a few minutes and gather her wits then step out into the dining room. As Chef of Total she had to make an appearance at the party and there was no way she could avoid facing Nestle Bingham and Rosamonde Beaudelaire.

The click-clack of dishes being washed, the sizzling of pans frying, and all of the other busy clatter of the kitchen faded into the background. Bella moved to each station and bent her head over each dish being prepared. With tunnel focus she smelled, tasted, and gave short words of encouragement and instruction, ignoring the twisting and turning of her stomach.

Everything had to be just right. Not only did she double check, she triple checked, and found that her staff had everything under control. She was almost sorry, for there was nothing else to do but face the food critic and her old boss.

She paused at the coat hooks lining the wall right next to the swinging door where all of the clean aprons hung and straightened her white frock and chef hat. She took a deep breath. She could do this. She had nothing to fear.

Bella turned away from the wall of aprons, ready to face her fate, and ran smack into a goofy, smiling reindeer named Dasher.

"Oof!" Mason said.

She wobbled, a little unsteady after running into him, from the mere sight of him. Looking up into his green eyes Bella felt her knees start to buckle.

They hadn't stood this close since Christmas Eve, which had been less than 24 hours before, but felt much longer. Eye level with his broad chest, she noted it was just as impressive in a reindeer shirt as it was in a tuxedo.

"Whoa," he said, grabbing her arms to steady her.

The touch of his fingers sent shivers up her arms and, apparently, numbed her tongue. She couldn't say anything. She blinked mutely up at him.

"Sorry," he said, his voice was so deep, so close, so husky.

He reached a hand up towards her face and Bella thought he was going to trace her cheek like he had the night before. She couldn't move. Didn't want to move. His hand didn't stop at her cheek, however, moving up to her hat instead. "I didn't mean to knock your hat off," he said as he adjusted her chef hat.

"Oh, right." She reached both hands up to fix it herself and their fingers brushed. Mason dropped his hand quickly. Heat rushed to her cheeks.

He cleared his throat. "I thought you should know Manuel's got everything moving over at our kitchen. Food is going up."

"The wedding's over?"

He nodded. "The ceremony is, I guess. Now they're eating."

"Oh, good, thank you for letting me know."

"Sure," he glanced around the busy kitchen.

Bella couldn't tear her eyes away from his handsome profile. When he looked back at her she realized she was staring. She averted her eyes.

"I was just going to check out the party," she said, looking past him towards the swinging doors.

"Of course," he stepped carefully around her so he could follow her out then remembered something. "Have you seen my Mom? She said she was coming over here."

"Yes, she was here," Bella replied. "I thought she was staying for the par–."

"Cake's going up!!" Posie called out through the open door of the walk-in refrigerator.

All eyes moved to the four waiters who were carefully maneuvering the four tiered black, red, and gold cake out of the refrigerator. Posie followed them carrying the top tier that would be placed when they got upstairs.

Activity in the kitchen ceased as they moved past the

sinks and stainless steel prep tables, avoiding the hot stove tops completely, then towards the swinging doors. Bella and Mason opened the doors and made sure the way was clear. As they held the doors open and the wedding cake passed between them, he caught her eye and held it. Transfixed, everything else blurred out of focus and all she could see was Mason, his mouth turned up in a cautious smile.

"Uh-oh, steady!" Posie's voice carried from the stairs.

Bella turned just in time to see the cake lurch and lean. They had begun their ascent of the stairs, taking the cake to the third floor banquet room while the wedding guests were being fed on the second floor. But the cake was tilted, not being held level, and it looked unnaturally crooked. She rushed to help, but the waiters had righted it by the time she reached the steps.

"Just take one step at a time, guys. Slow and steady," Posie instructed, giving Bella a comical look of horror.

Bella laughed, relieved. Even though they had a backup cake, avoiding a wedding cake drop down the stairs would be ideal. She turned back to Mason to see his reaction, but he was gone. Her momentary good mood dulled.

Needing a moment to compose herself, Bella took a few deep breaths and straightened her smock and hat again. She still had to find Nestle and Rosamonde. No time to fret over Mason disappearing.

Bella scanned the busy dining room, taking in for the first time how many guests had arrived when she was busy in the kitchen. The room was crowded, but full of fun. Christmas music played over the speakers, but it could barely be heard above the animated conversations and laughter. Lights twinkled, glasses clinked, and Bella could hardly believe this was her restaurant. Total. So full of life and good food and drink. The party appeared to be a success.

Bella climbed to the third step for a better vantage point.

She wanted to find Noah and ask him how Nestle and Rosamonde were getting along before she spoke to them. She searched the crowded party for Noah's dark beard and round glasses. Unfortunately, there were several men in the room with a similar look. There was, however, only one man who towered over the others.

Mason.

He was at the bar sipping a beer and looking a little bit like a giant elf in his reindeer shirt. A giant, gorgeous elf.

Bella's heart fluttered. He was talking and smiling. Seeing him so at ease made her regret how she had spurned him under the tree.

She wondered what would it be like to have someone like Mason as her boyfriend. Someone strong and kind, fun and generous, tall and handsome. Someone confident and charming who could talk with anybody. He was making conversation as she watched, she could see the way the two people at the bar next to him were engaged by him. They laughed and nodded and chatted happily. The man was bald with a thin nose and glasses. The woman was big busted and threw her head back when she laughed.

Suddenly, Bella recognized them both and all good vibes vanished.

CHAPTER 26

Mason was chatting it up with none other than Nestle Bingham and Rosamonde Baudelaire at the bar.

"No, no, no," she whispered. What was he saying to them? She couldn't allow any kind of misunderstandings or problems. Not after all of their hard work getting ready for this party. She had to intervene immediately.

Before she stepped down, something else caught her eye and she turned to see Noah waving at her from the front of the restaurant. She waved back and jabbed a finger towards Mason at the bar, indicating Noah should meet her there. Then Bella plunged into the crowd and pressed through.

"That's what I told her!" Mason was saying just as Bella emerged from the crowd surrounding him, Nestle, and Rosamonde.

"You did not!" Rosamonde laughed again, a great big hoarse laugh that erupted from her throat as she threw her head back.

Nestle Bingham snickered and covered his mouth with a

napkin. He was holding a plate with two spicy garlic shrimp, a half of a goat cheese croquette and two churros dribbled in chocolate glaze. Chewing on the other half of the croquette and trying not to laugh, he pressed the napkin more firmly over his mouth. Bella was immediately worried he might choke.

The potential headline New York Times Food Critic Dies at Total entered her mind and she glared at Mason.

Mason's face lit up when he saw her. Ignoring her nasty look, he reached out his hand, welcoming her into their conversation. "Bella, there you are."

Nestle and Rosamonde both turned to her and Bella didn't know which was worse, trying to think of something to say to the food critic she barely knew or the television producer she knew altogether too well.

Fortunately, perhaps, she was saved the trouble of what to say by the re-appearance of Mrs. Povich.

"Son! I've been looking for you," Mrs. Povich said as pushed her way in next to Mason. Their matching reindeer shirts must have made an impression on Nestle, he lifted the other half of his croquette into the air in an informal toast when he saw them. "Guess who I've met?" Mrs. Povich asked Mason excitedly.

The answer to her question appeared suddenly by her side. Tall, faux-blonde, red gown, Georgina's mother was apparently Mason's mother's new acquaintance.

"So, you're Mason," Georgina's mother gushed. She patted him right on the chest as if she was petting the forehead of his cartoon reindeer. "I remember you. You're the hunk-a-munk-a."

Bella didn't understand what was happening. Where had Mrs. Povich met Georgina's mother? What was going on upstairs at the wedding?

"And Bella!" Georgina's mother turned her attention to

her. She was a little wobbly. A little drunk. "Bella that cake is absolutely divine. Isn't it?" She directed that question back to Mrs. Povich.

"Absolutely divine," Mrs. Povich repeated, her red apple cheeks glowing.

Bella was trying to put together how Mason's mother had seen Georgina's wedding cake. She caught Mason watching her, noticing her confusion.

"Ma, were you upstairs?" he asked.

"Oh, sweetie, I was just looking around," his mother answered with a swish of her hand, shooing away any possibility of a reprimand. "We only snuck a tiny bit of the cake."

Georgina's mother nodded reassuringly and whispered, "Only a teeny weeny taste."

"Bella," Rosamonde had sidled up to the other side of her while she was distracted by Mrs. Povich.

"Hi Rosamonde, how are you?" Bella tried to sound calm and collected.

"I'm good, really good. But you, my dear, you have been busy haven't you?" Rosamonde let her eyes wander around the festivities surrounding them. The Christmas party-goers were obviously enjoying themselves.

"A little," Bella replied, happy that Rosamonde seemed to have her claws retracted on this night.

"So, there's cake?" Nestle asked.

Noah, who had arrived in their little circle by the bar without Bella noticing, chimed in, "There's a wedding in the upstairs banquet rooms today."

Nestle lifted his eyebrows in what Bella hoped was impressed surprise.

"My daughter's wedding!" Georgina's mother announced. "Where's my champagne?" She looked around as if she had been holding champagne and dropped it.

"Allow me," Nestle leaned over the bar since he was the

closest and waved at the bartender. "A champagne please, along with my wine." He gave the rest of them a questioning look, an unspoken invitation to order them champagne as well.

"I'll have one!" Mrs. Povich said.

Mason glanced at Bella with the same awkward embarrassment he'd had when they were in his mother's cramped living room. But Bella was too tense to respond. Her stomach was roiling with tension and it was taking everything in her power to keep up a facade of calm competence. Rosamonde remained at her side and she was just waiting for her old producer to whisper something mean or insulting into her ear.

Then there was Nestle Bingham who placidly handed out the two glasses of champagne to the older women then picked up a glass of red wine that the bartender gave him. Except it wasn't the bartender. Not her bartender, Flynn. It was Mark, the Mark from Pits who she had hired to help decorate.

Bella frowned in confusion. Why was Mark bartending?

"What's this?" Nestle asked, he was also frowning. He had just taken a sip of his wine and was making a sour face at Mark behind the bar. "I ordered a Syrah...this is Merlot."

All eyes in their small circle turned to Mark, who was now just as confused as Nestle, even more. Bella's stomach hardened into a knot.

"Do you keep a Syrah?" Nestle turned on Bella with the question and all eyes shifted to her. She tried to think, they must have Syrah, but her mind was blank. Flynn would know. But where was Flynn? Bella knew she could normally handle this type of situation smoothly, but staring into the bespectacled eyes of the prim Nestle Bingham filled her with doubt.

"Yes, of course we have Syrah," Noah announced. He looked to Mark who seemed even more confused.

Nobody moved. There was a long, awkward pause where nobody said anything, then Mason's deep, confident voice took over.

"Mark's covering for the regular bartender while he went on break. I'm sure Flynn will be back in a minute and get you the right wine."

Nestle sniffed and glanced into his wine glass, disappointed. His disappointment filled Bella with dread.

"Bella...er...Ms. Velez has hired quite a few new people to help over the holidays," Mason seemed to be the only person who could think of anything to say. "To help with the party and the wedding...people that needed the work."

"Really?" Rosamonde seemed interested in that fact, or maybe she was just interested in Mason, Bella wasn't sure.

"Yes, ma'am," Mark answered, eager to atone for his wine mistake. "My wife and I have been out of work for several months now and Ms. Velez hired us both to help decorate for the wedding."

"And where did you meet?" Rosamonde continued her inquiry.

"We were helping Mason and Eddie next door at Pits...for the free Christmas dinner," Mark answered.

"Free Christmas dinner?" Nestle seemed interested.

"Oh, yes! Henrietta told me all about that," Georgina's mother chimed in.

"Henrietta?" Bella asked, trying to wrap her mind around the conversation.

Georgina's mother pointed her already half empty champagne glass at Mrs. Povich. "Henrietta told me all about how her son and his restaurant gave away hundreds and hundreds of free turkey and ham dinners today. So generous!"

"There you are!" Charlotte exclaimed as she pushed her way into their conversation circle. Looking past the rest of them, she zeroed in on Georgina's mother. "They're going to cut the cake soon."

Georgina's mother raised her glass in a happy salute. "You'll have to excuse me, I've been summoned by Mr. and Mrs. R.C. Reynolds!" She gulped down the last half of her champagne.

Nestle Bingham gave her a curious look. "*The* R.C. Reynolds?"

"The one and only. He's my new son-in-law," she grinned at Nestle then had a thought and touched Bella's arm. "He would be very interested in all of this. He's quite a philanthropist, you know." She gave Bella a wink and took Mason's mother by the arm. "Come on, Henrietta, let's try some more of that amazing wedding cake."

Bella watched Charlotte lead the two older women back through the crowded party towards the stairway, still uncertain what exactly had happened. She felt a nudge in her side. Rosamonde.

"That's quite an angle you've got going on," Rosamonde said with an appreciative sly wink.

"Angle?"

"Yes, helping the needy and hosting the wedding of one of the richest men in the city on the same day–Christmas Day. It's quite a story." Rosamonde lifted her glass and took a knowing sip.

"Story?" Bella knew that she was just repeating words as questions, but no other response came to mind. She looked at Noah, who was both listening to Rosamonde and surreptitiously watching Nestle Bingham. He caught her eye and gave her a discreet, hopeful thumbs up.

"Here's your Syrah, sir," Mason announced from the bar. Flynn had returned and poured the right drink.

"Thank you," Nestle said. He put his empty plate and the

partly drank glass of Merlot on the bar to pick up his new drink. When he turned back from the bar he looked straight at Bella and raised his wine glass. "The Merlot was quite good, actually, as was the food. My compliments."

All of the talking and laughing and music in the room blended together and rose to a crescendo in her ears. Had she heard him correctly? She stared into the food critic's pale blue eyes and saw the hint of a smile as he watched her for a reaction. That hint was enough.

Relief. Gratitude. Joy. All three filled her up, replacing the anxiety she had been feeling ever since she read his first review in the Times weeks ago. Despite the massive emotional shift happening inside her body, she managed to maintain her composure and returned his smile with a gracious, "Thank you."

Suddenly, the sounds of the room became clear again. Bella could hear everything. The nearby conversations and laughter. The clinking of glasses and dishes as people enjoyed Total's food. The Christmas music playing over the speakers. Deck the Halls, an oldie but a goodie.

Mason remained next to the bar, his silly reindeer shirt seemed happily appropriate now that Bella's worries about Nestle and Rosamonde had lifted. He watched her with his own smiling eyes, the twinkle had returned, happy that she was happy. Mason cocked his head, pretending to hear the music for the first time.

"Deck the halls with boughs of holly..." his clear, strong voice rang out above the rest of the sounds of the party and people looked his way. Mason lifted his glass high into the air, taking advantage of his height, and began conducting as he sang. "Fa-la-la-la-la-la-la-la-la!"

Other voices joined his, "Tis the season to be jolly, fa-la-la-la-la-la-la-la-la!"

Noah clinked his glass against Mason's and sang. Mark helped Lynn wipe down the bar and sang. Rosamonde swayed back and forth and sang. Everyone sang. Even Nestle Bingham. And, after wiping a few happy tears from her eyes, Bella sang along with them all.

CHAPTER 27

"Success!" Posie cried out as she locked the front door behind the very last of the staff and guests.

Bella laughed, "It's a Christmas miracle!"

"A toast?" Noah held up a bottle of champagne.

"Yes, please," Charlotte answered.

It was almost midnight and the four of them plus Davis, Manuel, Eddie, and Mason were all who remained in the entire restaurant. The wedding was over, the party was over, but Bella's career as a New York City restauranteur was just beginning. Exhausted, spent, dead on her feet, she was happier than she had been in a long time.

"I can't tell you all how grateful I am for everything you've done," she said as Noah handed out champagne for the toast.

Davis raised his glass first. "We were happy to be part of this, Bella."

"It's what friends do," Charlotte added.

"To good friends!" Posie exclaimed.

"To good food," Manuel added.

"To Christmas!" Eddie chimed in.

"Merry Christmas," Bella smiled.

They all repeated, "Merry Christmas!" Clinked glasses and drank.

It was time to go. The only thing left to do was turn off the lights and lock up. Noah, Posie, and Manuel left together. As they passed in front of Total's front picture window, snow began to fall. Soft flakes drifting lightly down through the final minutes of Christmas were the final touch of magic. Bella smiled as she watched from the front cashier counter.

"I guess that's a night," Mason said from behind.

Her heartbeat quickened as he stepped up to her side, keeping his eyes on the snow falling outside.

"Yes, it's all over. I can hardly believe it," she said.

They stayed like that for a long moment, side-by-side, quiet together, until Mason asked, "Are you happy, Bella?"

Bella looked up to find him watching her instead of the snow. Her heart skipped a beat at the look in his eyes. Sweet, caring...sad.

"With the way everything turned out?" he added quickly.

Unable to answer him while gazing into his eyes, Bella turned to the cash register as if she was going to finish up counting receipts from the day, even though she knew there were none to count. Something–anything–to distract her from his presence, the sheer closeness of his body to hers.

"Sure, yes, absolutely. It's all turned out so much better than I thought it could." She hurriedly opened the cash drawer and, pretending to not find what she was looking for, slammed it shut again.

Maybe she slammed it much harder than she meant to and caused a vibration through the nearby decorations, or maybe Christmas was over and the Christmas Spider knew its job was done, but for some unknown reason the shimmering arachnid slipped slightly off the garland and dropped down, dangling from one of its sparkling feet, catching their attention.

Bella reached up and took the Christmas Spider down before it fell. She considered it for a moment and looked up at Mason. "I think this poor thing is worn out. It had a lot of work to do getting me through this holiday." Mason grinned and she felt a little weak in the knees at the sight. Bella handed him the decoration. "You should take him back now so he can rest up for next year."

Their fingers brushed as he took the Christmas Spider from her and she remembered when he first brought the decorations over. How smitten she had been by his good looks. How surprised at his thoughtfulness.

"Yeah, thanks. I'll put him away until next year," Mason answered, turning the spider over in his hands.

"You ready?" Eddie asked as he came to the front of the restaurant.

"Um, yeah..." Mason looked uncomfortable. He directed his gaze back at her, "Do you need a lift home...or anything?"

She shook her head, "No, thank you. I'll go with Charlotte and Davis." As the words left her mouth she was sorry. She wouldn't have minded his company. She didn't know why she always had to say 'no' right away.

"Okay...okay, well, good night," Mason said, giving her a parting wave with the Christmas Spider in hand.

She remained at the cash register and watched him and Eddie walk away. Mason glanced back once and she turned away quickly, pushing buttons on the cash register so he wouldn't know she had been watching, making the drawer pop open again. The empty spot the Christmas Spider had occupied seemed blank and dull. Everything else suddenly seemed blank and dull.

Bella closed the drawer to the cash register, pressing it

slowly into place until she felt it click. Her shoulders sank as she stood there, silent, nothing to do. With the events over and the holiday over Bella realized she didn't have anything more to think about...or look forward to either.

Hot tears burned the back of her eyes and she tried to blink them away, but they had surfaced too fast. It was all she could do to choke back an audible sob as they flowed uncontrollably down her cheeks.

"Hey, are you okay?"

Bella whirled around to find Davis moving cautiously to her side. She shook her head 'no', because she couldn't speak a word, afraid she would start sobbing instead.

"What happened?" Davis put an arm protectively around her shoulders and scanned the room for someone to blame for her break down.

But there was nobody to blame, Bella knew, unless she was willing to be honest and blame herself.

"I–I–I..." she stuttered as she tried to explain and the stutter turned into blubbering.

"I'm gonna get Charlotte," Davis said.

Bella shook her head back and forth more vehemently. Charlotte would fuss too much.

"Are you sure?" Davis looked pained and more than a little uncomfortable.

Bella nodded and wiped her nose with the back of her hand. He grabbed a cloth napkin from where they kept the extra silverware under the cash register and handed it to her.

"I'm sorry," Bella said, blowing her nose.

"Don't be sorry," he patted her back. "Do you want to talk about it?"

"I think I'm just overwhelmed, you know. Feeling sad that everything's over...everybody's gone..."

Davis watched her thoughtfully as she blew her nose again

then he bent his head towards her so he could speak quietly, "Anyone in particular?"

Bella winced, disappointed that all attempts to remain aloof had been a waste of time. "Is it that obvious?"

Davis shook his head 'no' then conceded, "No, no, not obvious...well, just a little bit obvious."

"Oh no," she groaned.

"Ah, I wouldn't worry about it. Not a big deal for people to be attracted to each other."

Bella gave him a dubious look and blew her nose again.

Davis smiled and leaned against the counter. He folded his arms in front of his chest like a teacher about to give an interesting lecture. "The only thing that would be a big deal was if two people had more than just attraction and let it slip away." He gave her a meaningful look. "I mean, if you and Ma—er, if two people had real feelings for each other that went past physical attraction and they ignored those feelings for...whatever reason." He shrugged as if trying to fathom a situation where two people who were in love didn't get together. "If they ignored those feelings and let someone special get away. Well, that would be a big deal if you ask me."

As his words sunk in, Bella was struck with a funny thought. "You sound just like Charlotte."

Davis smiled, "My wife's a smart woman."

Her tears gone, she sniffled and wiped her eyes with the edge of the napkin. "I guess...I'm not sure if he has those real feelings for me."

Davis stood and looked over his shoulder at the front door where Mason had walked out just a few minutes before. He turned back to her with an encouraging smile, "There's only one way to find out."

It took no time at all for Bella to reach the front door of Pits. All of the hope and anticipation of seeing Mason, of telling him how she felt about him, swirled inside of her and made it seem like she was floating on air. The thrill of possibility pounded in her heart.

She tried the handle, it was locked. Of course, they weren't open. The lights were all off inside. Even as she peeked through cupped hands against the window into the dark restaurant she knew he wasn't there. It was almost midnight on Christmas and he had already gone home.

Her excitement to see him sank into dismay. Every other triumph of the night faded away. Christmas was almost over and she was overwhelmed with a need to see Mason in the last moments of this magical day.

She sighed, defeated. The wet snow dropped out of the sky, soaking into her hair and clothes. She hadn't put on a coat. With a shiver, Bella wrapped her arms around herself and turned to go back to Total, and back home, and back to her life, without seeing him, not knowing if she would have the courage to tell him how she felt the next time she saw him. For her, everything hinged on the magic of this moment...and the magic was gone.

Christmas was over and so was their working together. Tomorrow would be a return to normal. She would be on her own again.

She was halfway back to Total when she heard his voice.

"Bella?"

Bella whirled around. He was there. Standing right there next to Pits' front door.

"I thought you were gone," she said, startled and breathless at his appearance.

"I was in the back." He took a few steps towards her and paused. "You're freezing. Where's your coat?"

"I'm fine, I wanted to see – to talk – I want to tell you something."

Mason came to her and took her by the elbow, turning her

towards Total's front door. "Okay, let's talk inside where it's warm."

Bella shook her arm away from him and stood stubbornly in the middle of the sidewalk. So many emotions filled her up and threatened to spill out in a confused mish-mash. Or worse, she might start crying.

"I don't want to go inside. I need to tell you something."

Mason stopped and gave her a cautious look. Seeing that she meant to stand in the middle of the falling snow and there was nothing he could do about it, he took off his coat and threw it around her shoulders.

"All right, we'll stay right here."

Under the weight of his coat Bella still couldn't put her words together.

Mason looked down into her eyes, curious and concerned, but waiting patiently.

Finally, Bella managed, "I–I never got to thank you for the tree. It's beautiful."

He took the compliment with confused amusement. "Oh, yeah. I ordered those a few weeks ago...before...you know..."

She did know. Before she had completely and successfully pushed him away. Bella tried to gather another sentence together while he waited, but her words remained jumbled and the snow kept falling. The last magical moments of Christmas were slipping away and would be gone soon. Fear that she would bungle the whole conversation and send him away again washed through her and she shivered.

"Was that what you wanted to say?" he asked.

"Yes. No. Not all of it."

"Okay," he glanced up into the night sky and the relentless snowflakes. "Are you sure you don't want to go inside?"

"I've made a mistake," she blurted out.

"A mistake?"

"Yes, a horrible, miserable mistake."

Mason's confusion returned. "What are you talking about? Everything went off with a bang. It was great. All of it. A Christmas miracle!" His eyes warmed as he smiled down at her. "You were amazing."

Bella gazed up at him, lost in those eyes, lost in him. "I couldn't have done it without you."

Mason dropped his gaze for a moment. He shook his head and started denying, "Naw, I didn't–"

Bella wouldn't let him finish. "I don't want to do it without you."

Mason lifted his gaze. Cautious again. When he spoke he chose his words carefully. "You don't want to do *what* without me?"

"Anything. Everything."

Still confused, but with a glimmer of hope in his eyes, he asked, "What are you saying?

Nervous butterflies exploding inside of her, Bella knew she had to make herself clear. She knew the time was now. She couldn't keep blundering around.

She reached out and took his hand. It was warm and strong and when he didn't pull it away, but wrapped it firmly around hers, she found the courage she needed.

"I was wrong to push you away. I was trying to deny my feelings because...I don't know why, exactly. Never mind. I do know. I'm scared. I'm scared of my feelings for you. I'm scared to make a mistake."

Bella stopped.

Mason held her gaze. He did not look away. He did not let go of her hand.

"Your feelings for me?"

"I'm not always nice, Mason. I'm not a delightful person to be around. I work too much. Sometimes I get angry. Sometimes I get worried–anxious. I can get really, really anxious and–and tense."

A twinkle entered his eyes as he watched her ramble on and on. When she was done he squeezed her hand and moved closer. "What feelings are we talking about exactly?"

Bella blushed. He took her other hand in his. Her knees felt weak as he moved even closer, his body against hers, warming her completely.

Her voice came out as a hoarse whisper, "I just don't want to mess this up."

Mason's voice was not a whisper. He was not afraid. "We're not going to get messed up. I promise."

Bella found comfort in that and leaned into him, letting his strength hold her up. He pulled her to him, let go of her hands and wrapped his arms around her body. She pressed her hands on him, but not to push away this time. Instead, she slid her hands up and over his muscled chest and around his neck, letting her fingertip gently trace the back of his neck.

"Bella," he whispered and leaned down, brushing his lips on her cheek.

"I'm falling for you," she said. His embrace tightened and she let her body sink into his. So warm. So strong.

"I've already fallen for you," he said softly into her ear.

His words tickled and she laughed in delight. When he pulled away to look down into her eyes, the old Mason was back. Laughter and love in his eyes and a smile on his lips.

Bella put her hand on his cheek, memorizing his face so she could always remember the moment that she fell in love. "It's another Christmas miracle! It must be your Christmas Spider," she said, smiling.

Suddenly, he moved his hands to her waist and lifted her into the air, giving her a twirl through the falling snow before setting her back down, his eyes shining.

"It is my Christmas Spider! He must have been working overtime for me in the background."

Bella laughed again. Joy filled her heart as she gazed up into the face of her love.

Mason lifted one hand and brushed a stray hair from her face. He leaned down, moving his mouth ever closer to her lips. Right before he kissed her he paused and said, "My miracle was always you."

CHAPTER 28

Dec. 26th - New York Times - Food - Restaurant Reviews

LAST NIGHT I had the sincere pleasure of attending a Christmas Party to end all Christmas parties.

Total, one of New York's newest dining gems, threw what can only be described as a complete holiday experience as their grand opening and I, humble food critic that I am, felt lucky to be invited.

The food was beyond delicious. The ambience was a perfect blend of every man authenticity and chic upper class. This mixture managed to give one the feeling of discovering something brand new while also being in a cozy much loved eatery. The holiday? Probably the nicest time I've had on Christmas Day in a very long time.

Chef Bella Velez has overcome her past and presented a future in Total that promises to bring New York uniquely delightful dining experiences that are not to be missed.

From perfect cheese croquettes and spicy shrimp cocktail to a delectable nibble of wedding cake from the nuptials of none other than

R.C Reynolds and his newest blushing bride, Georgina Andreanakis, who celebrated their marriage in Total's intimate upstairs banquet rooms, every dish was prepared perfectly.

Beyond perfection, actually, because the food was prepared, in my opinion, with the one ingredient missing in so many dishes these days, the one ingredient that has no substitution—love.

MERRY CHRISTMAS,
   - Nestle Bingham

THANK you for reading Bella's Christmas Blunder! You may like another of Darci Balogh's Christmas books, Mistletoe Madness, the third book in her Sweet Holiday Romance series.

Go to www.knowheremedia.com/books to find out more!

ABOUT THE AUTHOR

Darci Balogh is an author and filmmaker who spent much of her life living both in and near the majestic Rocky Mountains of Colorado.

She now resides in the beautiful state of Michigan near Lake Huron. She has two amazing grown daughters, too many dogs, and an aversion to dusting.

Her fiction is a blend of women's fiction and romance (both sweet and spicy) with strong female characters and charming leading men. She has been a writer since she was a child and enjoys crafting stories into novels and screenplays.

Big surprise, some of her favorite pastimes are reading and watching movies. Classic British TV is high on her 'Like' list, along with quietly depressing detective series all while sipping coffee with heavy cream.

www.ingramcontent.com/pod-product-compliance
Lightning Source LLC
Chambersburg PA
CBHW020801190726
48285CB00006B/2130